There was definite

Something she'd done have.

Something...

Wait a minute.

Images from the night before flashed through her mind.

The Italian place. She'd had a little too much Chianti, hadn't she? And then, in the limo, sailing along the strip, making love. Drinking champagne.

But the champagne was no excuse. She hadn't been *that* drunk. She'd been perfectly cognizant of everything that happened.

When they'd just *happened* to stop at the place you get a marriage license, what had she done? Followed him in like a lamb to the slaughter.

And when he'd whipped the ring out of his pocket, had she said, "Declan Keallach McGrath, you hold on just a minute here. What is that ring doing in your pocket?"

No, she had not.

Instead, she'd let him take her hand and slip that ring onto her finger. And then she'd clung to him like paint as they'd rolled on down the strip to that wedding place called Now and Forever.

Now and Forever.

Oh, my God.

The mermaid wedding dress. The flowers. The Gardenia Chapel...

Sweet Lord in heaven.

What had she done?

THE BRAVOS OF JUSTICE CREEK:
Where bold hearts collide under Western skies

Dear Reader,

One of my favorite things about writing and reading romances is that, in a romance, the hero and heroine never give up. No matter the obstacles in their path, one way or another they will make it through to find each other by the time the story reaches its end.

Declan McGrath is proud and relentless and often thickheaded. He lost brave, beautiful, fiercely loyal Nell Bravo eleven years ago and he has no one to blame but himself for that loss. Nell has sworn never to go near Deck again.

But Deck has finally seen the light. He knows now that Nell is the woman for him, and he's determined to make her his, no matter what he has to do to make that happen.

He's been pursuing her for months now. On a tip from her matchmaking mother, he follows Nell when she heads for Las Vegas to attend a trade show. There, he pulls out all the stops with her to get one more chance.

But Nell is not won yet. It's going to take the whole Christmas season and all the love in his heart to make her see that they were meant to be together.

Merry Christmas, everyone. I hope Nell and Deck's story helps put you in the holiday spirit, and I wish you a beautiful Christmas season and love and happiness in the New Year.

All my very best,

Christine Rimmer

Married
Till Christmas

———

Christine Rimmer

HARLEQUIN® SPECIAL EDITION®

Recycling programs
for this product may
not exist in your area.

ISBN-13: 978-0-373-62386-0

Married Till Christmas

Printed in U.S.A.

www.Harlequin.com

Christine Rimmer came to her profession the long way around. She tried everything from acting to teaching to telephone sales. Now she's finally found work that suits her perfectly. She insists she never had a problem keeping a job—she was merely gaining "life experience" for her future as a novelist. Christine lives with her family in Oregon. Visit her at christinerimmer.com.

Books by Christine Rimmer

Harlequin Special Edition

The Bravos of Justice Creek

Garrett Bravo's Runaway Bride
The Lawman's Convenient Bride
A Bravo for Christmas
Ms. Bravo and the Boss
James Bravo's Shotgun Bride
Carter Bravo's Christmas Bride
The Good Girl's Second Chance
Not Quite Married

Montana Mavericks: The Great Family Roundup

The Maverick Fakes a Bride!

Montana Mavericks: The Baby Bonanza

Marriage, Maverick Style!

Montana Mavericks: What Happened at the Wedding?

The Maverick's Accidental Bride

Visit the Author Profile page
at Harlequin.com for more titles.

For my family, with all my love.

Chapter One

"God, you are beautiful. That red hair, those big green eyes. That amazing body. And those lips. Baby, those lips were made for a man to bite. Can I tell you a secret?"

Nell Bravo had a one-word answer for that one. "No."

But the handsome guy in the expensive suit wasn't listening. He leaned extra close, breathing Booker's Rye—and no, he wasn't really drunk, only buzzed enough to get pushy. "I don't usually go for tattoos on a woman." He eyed the half sleeve of bright ink that swirled over her left arm from shoulder to elbow. "But, in your case, I'm definitely making an exception. I'd like to jump you right here at the bar."

Nell considered summoning the energy to be offended, but that would be faking it. She'd never minded the brash approach, not as long as she was interested. Too bad she just wasn't—and hadn't been for a long time now.

Except for one man.

One man who managed to show up every time she turned around lately, a guy she was not letting close to her ever again, thank you very much—and that did it. That finished it. She'd had enough of the handsome fellow in the pricey suit.

Not only did he refuse to take a hint, he'd gone and made her think of the one person she wanted nothing to do with.

Ever again.

Not even in her mind.

Somewhere behind her, bells and whistles went off as a lucky slot player hit a jackpot. Nell grabbed her clutch, whipped out a twenty and slid it under her cocktail napkin for the bartender. "That's it for me."

"Whoa now," said the guy beside her, whose name was Ron. "Put your money away."

"Great to meet you, Ron," she lied. "I've got your card and I'll be in touch." He owned Ron's Custom Tile, with five stores in the Bay Area and Los Angeles. Her company, Bravo Construction, ordered a lot of tile. Maybe they could have done some business. Probably not now, though. Ron was just way too interested in looking down her dress. "Good night." She spun on her stool, lowered her Jimmy Choos to the floor and set off for the lobby area and the elevator up to her room.

But Ron was no quitter. "Hold on a minute." He was right behind her. "Baby, don't go…"

Nell stopped in her tracks. When she turned, he almost plowed into her. "Look." She pinned him with her coldest stare. "I don't know how much clearer I can make this. I'm not interested in being jumped by you—right there at the bar, or anywhere in else in this hotel. Good night, Ron."

He started to speak again, but she didn't hang around to hear it. Instead, she took off, moving faster now, weaving her way past the rows of whizzing, dinging slot machines and on to the never-ending main casino floor. She flew past the gaming tables and more bars and restaurants, her high heels tapping hard over polished floors, ears tuned for the sound of Ron's footsteps behind her.

Yep. The idiot was following her.

So what? He wasn't going to catch her. She kept going, never once looking back.

Finally, she reached the blue-lit hotel lobby with its glittering waterfall wall and swirling peacock-colored carpet. As she veered by the concierge desk, she slipped her key card from her clutch.

Entering the marble-lined bank of elevators at last, she pushed the button to go up.

Unfortunately, no car was available.

Crap. Okay, she could just keep on going out the other end of the bay and circle back around, hoping to lose Ron in the process.

Or simply wait.

Screw it. She waited, which gave Ron the chance to catch up with her. When he reached her, she glanced the other way. Maybe ignoring him would do the trick.

Not so much. He grabbed her arm and pulled her around to face him. "Now, just a damn minute here."

"Ron. You don't look all that handsome with that mean scowl on your face."

"I just want to—"

"No, Ron. I said no."

"There's no need to be rude, Nell." He spoke through clenched teeth and he still had a death grip on her arm.

Nell felt a burning need to give Ron the sharp knee in the family jewels he very much deserved. But she kept her cool. "Seriously, Ron? This is going nowhere good. It's a casino, in case you didn't notice." She pointed at the camera mounted up where the wall met the ceiling. "The eye-in-the-sky sees all. I only need to let out a scream and your evening will be downgraded from bad to a whole lot worse."

His grip on her arm loosened. Before she could congratulate herself for some smooth handling of an iffy situation, she noticed that Ron's narrowed eyes had widened and shifted upward toward something behind her.

Yanking her arm free, she turned.

Not possible. "Deck?" It couldn't be.

Oh, but it was. Declan McGrath, all six foot four and two-hundred-plus muscled-up pounds of him, right here in Vegas. At *her* hotel.

"What a coincidence running into you here," said Deck in that rough, low, wonderful voice of his.

Nell rolled her eyes so hard she almost fell over. "Coincidence, my ass. Don't even try to tell me you're here for the Worldwide Hard Surfaces Trade Show."

"Okay, I won't." The corners of his mouth inched upward in the slow, delicious smile that used to make her life worth living. Years and years ago. Back when she was young and trusting, before he'd dumped her flat—twice. "God, Sparky. You do look good."

She gave him the same look she'd been giving Ron—a look of ice and steel. "How many times do I have to say it? Don't call me Sparky."

"I just can't help myself."

"You don't *want* to help yourself."

"That's right. I never give up. And we both know it's just a matter of time until you give in and give me a break."

"You're delusional."

"I prefer to call it thinking positive."

"Hold on just a damn minute," Ron piped up from behind her. "What the hell is going on here?"

Nell turned to tell the tile man—again—to get lost.

But Deck stepped around her and took Ron's arm.

Ron flailed. "What the hell, man? Let go of my arm."

"In a minute." Deck glanced back to pin Nell with a look. "Do. Not. Move." And then he pulled Ron down to the other end of the enclosure and whispered something in his ear. Ron paled.

The nearest elevator dinged and the doors slid open. Several people filed out. Nell watched them go, thinking that she should get on and get away before Deck came back.

But then again, no. Just no. She'd been walking away from Deck for months now. Enough of that. This time he'd finally gone too far.

Following her to Vegas? Who *did* that?

She wasn't surrendering the field this time. Not until she'd treated him to a very large piece of her mind. And maybe the kick in the cojones she'd almost given Ron.

More elevator cars arrived and more people spilled out as Deck whispered in Ron's ear.

"Got it," said Ron, blond head bobbing. "Loud and clear."

"Fair enough." Deck let go of his arm.

Ron backed away with both hands up. "But hey, like I said, she's not wearing a ring."

"A ring?" Nell demanded. Not that either man was listening.

"She's naughty like that sometimes," Deck said with a so-what shrug. "Now get lost." Ron didn't argue. He took off. Nell leaned against the marble wall, her arms crossed over her chest, as Deck turned her way again. "Good," he said. "You're still here."

Where to even start with him? "You've got to leave me alone, Deck."

He came toward her, so big and solid, all lazy male grace, in jeans that hugged his hard legs and an olive-green shirt that made his hazel eyes gleam so damn bright—chameleon eyes, she used to call them. They seemed different colors depending on his mood and the light. He'd rolled his sleeves to his elbows, showing off strong forearms, all muscled and veiny, dusted with sandy-colored hair.

It just wasn't fair. No man should be allowed to look that amazing. She wrapped her arms tighter around herself to keep her grabby hands from reaching out and squeezing those rock-hard muscles of his.

Because, she bleakly reminded herself, squeezing Deck's muscles—or any other part of him, for that matter—was a big, fat never-again.

He kept on coming. She had to put up a hand. "That's close enough."

"I love that red dress. You should wear red all the time."

"I know, I know. Goes with my hair, blah, blah, blah. Did you tell Ron we're married?"

He smirked. "Worked, didn't it?"

"Except, well, doesn't that make me the kind of woman who takes off her wedding ring and goes trolling for a hot date with a stranger?"

Deck snorted. "Ron? Hot?"

"Well, theoretically speaking—and Ron's hotness or lack thereof? Totally not the issue here."

"Sparky," he chided. "You would never cheat, I know that. The thing with Ron was only to make me jealous."

Two elevators opened at the same time. People got off and others got on.

She waited till the doors slid shut to say, "There *was* no thing with Ron. And what do you mean, make you jealous? I had no idea you were in Vegas, and even if I'd known you'd followed me here, I would have zero desire to make you jealous."

"But you did make me jealous. And I forgive you. You're a high-spirited woman, always have been. You've got to have your fun."

Where was this going? Somehow, once again with him, she was failing to make the point that he should give up chasing after her because she was never getting caught—not by him. No way. "I think it's just possible that you've finally completely lost your mind."

He slapped both big hands against his chest. "Go ahead. Hurt me. Call me names. I can take it."

More elevator doors opened. If she ducked into one, he would probably just follow her. Dropping her key card into her clutch, she drew away from the wall and started walking backward. Deck came after her. They ended up facing off by a potted ficus plant around the corner from the constant flow of people going up and down floors.

"What now, Nellie?" he asked, his voice so gentle suddenly, the intimate sound tugging on a tender place inside her, a place she used to be so certain he had killed stone dead all those years ago.

Why wouldn't it die? This...*feeling* she had for him, this stupid, impossible yearning for a man who had turned his back on her twice after promising she would always be the only one for him?

He just stood there now, close enough to reach out and touch, waiting for her to make her next move. Oh, she just ached to open her mouth and yell at him to leave her alone, get the hell away from her. But yelling would not only bring security running, it would be admitting that he was actually getting to her.

Which he was. And which he knew already. She could see that in his gleaming, watchful eyes.

It was bad enough that he knew. Losing her temper over it would only prove how powerfully he affected her. "Who told you I would be here?"

"Have dinner with me and we can talk about that." He took a step closer.

"Forget dinner." She stepped back. The ficus tree was right behind her. A trailing branch brushed her shoulder. "And I already know the answer to my question. Garrett told you I was here, am I right?" Her brother and partner in Bravo Construction *liked* Deck, damn it. Plus, there was the big, high-end house Deck had hired BC to build. Generally speaking, it was good business for Garrett to help an important client get what he wanted—but not when what he wanted was another chance with Nell. Garrett had no right to take a customer's side against his business partner, who also happened to be his own flesh and blood. "I'm going to kill Garrett."

Deck stuck his hands in his pockets. She read the move as an attempt to look easygoing and harmless. As if. "It wasn't Garrett," he said.

"Then who?"

"Your mother told me."

Now Nell *really* wanted to start yelling. Willow Bravo had turned into a matchmaking nightmare over the past couple of years. She'd become obsessed with seeing her children married and settled down. At least until now Willow had shown the good sense to leave Nell out of all that crap.

But, one by one, Willow's other four grown children had found marital bliss. That meant only Nell remained single and Willow just couldn't let well enough alone.

"You pumped my mother for information about me?" Nell kept her voice low, but barely.

"Whoa. Settle down."

"That's just plain wrong."

"True," he said with zero remorse. "When it comes to you, I'll do whatever I have to do. But I didn't go to your mother. *She* called *me*. She said she hasn't forgotten how much you loved me once."

Nell pressed her lips together and expelled an outraged breath through her nose. "Admit it. She called you after you let her know that you've been trying to get something going with me."

"Think about it, Nellie." He looked way too pleased with himself. "How could she *not* know that I've been chasing you?"

He had a point.

In recent months, Deck had made himself famous in their hometown of Justice Creek with his relentless pursuit of her. He'd started his campaign to get her attention by going to the places she went—her brother Quinn's fitness center, her half sister Elise's bakery for coffee early in the morning and her friend Rye McKellan's pub. His constant presence at McKellan's had really annoyed her. She not only liked to hang out there—she lived above the pub in the loft next door to Rye's.

After a month or so of turning up just about everywhere she went, he'd called her and asked her straight out for a date.

She'd said, "Absolutely not and do not call me again."

He hadn't called again. But he *had* shown up at Bravo Construction to ask her to build his new house. She'd handed him over to Garrett.

Then he'd begun showering her with flowers and gifts. She'd refused to accept them. He'd hired a skywriter to blaze their names in a heart across the Colorado sky. She'd pretended not to notice.

Every time he would come up with a new way to get her attention, she would shut him right down. She'd never imagined he'd follow her all the way to Sin City.

Yet, here he was again.

"I'll be having a serious talk with my mother," she

said. "And you should be ashamed of yourself, pumping her for information about my whereabouts when I have told you repeatedly that once was more than enough when it comes to you—I mean, twice when you count how you came back to me after breaking up with me, only to break up with me all over again."

"I'll say it once more. I didn't pump your mother for information. She called me and volunteered it. And as for me dumping you, that was more than a decade ago. It was high school. We were only kids. I was messed up and not ready. We're different people now."

"No, we're not. I'm still the girl who would have taken a bullet for your sorry ass. And you're the guy who fooled me twice. That's two times too many." And yet, here she was, backed up against a ficus tree, arguing with him when there was supposed to be nothing she had to say to him.

And he still wouldn't give it up. "If you won't have dinner with me, how about a drink? We can discuss how much you despise me in comfort—and in depth."

"I never said I despise you," she muttered grudgingly. Was she weakening? Oh, all right. Maybe a little. She added more firmly, "You just need to catch a flight back to Justice Creek and leave me the hell alone."

"One drink, Nell." The man had some kind of radar. He knew he was getting to her. "One drink won't kill you. And I get it. You don't want to be seen out with me. You don't want anyone to imagine you might be thinking of giving me another chance."

"Because I'm not."

"But look at it this way." He lowered his already velvety tone even more, down to an intimate, just-you-

and-me growl. "This is Vegas and you've heard what they say about Vegas. No one ever has to know…"

It was a really bad idea and she needed to walk away.

But she just couldn't help comparing him to Ron the tile man—to every man she met, as a matter of fact. He wasn't the guy for her, but he was kind of her gold standard of what a man should be—well, aside from the way he'd smashed her heart to bits two times running.

No, she couldn't trust him. But he was hot and funny and smart. He was that perfect combination, the one she couldn't resist: a big, down-to-earth blue-collar guy with a really sharp brain. And he'd been after her for months now.

Okay, it made her feel like a fool to admit it, but lately she'd been having these crazy urges to go ahead and let him catch her.

She wouldn't, of course. He would never catch her again.

But it was Friday night in Vegas, and going back to her room seemed beyond depressing. Friday night in the second week of November and she was alone when all of her siblings were happily married—half siblings, too—and there were four of those.

She was the only single Bravo left in Justice Creek. Too soon, it would be Thanksgiving and then it would be Christmas, with all those family get-togethers where everyone would be coupled up but her. Even her aggravating widowed mother was getting remarried.

And, one of these days, Nell wanted to be married, too.

Unfortunately, only once in her life had she found a

guy who really made it happen for her. That guy was standing in front of her now. And he just wouldn't let it go. He kept coming after her. With him constantly popping up every time she turned around, how was she supposed to stop comparing every guy she met to him?

It just wasn't right. It needed to stop.

But running away from him had gotten her nowhere.

"One drink, Nellie," he said again, his voice a rough-tender temptation, his eyes eating her up and, at the same time, daring her to look away.

What could it hurt, really? Maybe she would actually get through to him at last.

Maybe tonight he would finally get the message. They could speak reasonably to each other and she could convince him to give up the chase. Come to think of it, she hadn't tried talking to him civilly, woman to man, yet. And walking away time after time just wasn't cutting it.

She sucked in a slow breath. "One drink."

For about half a second, he looked totally stunned, the way he had all those years and years ago, when she'd taken the desk in front of him the first day of sophomore English and then turned around and grinned at him. He'd gaped at her, his expression one of complete shock. But only for a moment. Then he'd looked away. She remembered staring at the side view of his Adam's apple, thinking he was hot, even though one of his battered sneakers had a hole in the toe, his shirt screamed hand-me-down and his hair looked like he'd cut it himself.

He was lean and rangy then, his shoulders broad

but not thick, more hungry-looking, like some wild animal, always ready to run. It had taken her weeks to get him to talk to her. And by then, she was a goner. She'd just known he was the guy for her.

Wrong.

The grown-up Deck had lost the stunned look. Once again, he was supremely confident, totally at ease. He said, "Well, all right then, Nellie. I know just the place."

Chapter Two

Declan McGrath had done what he set out to do. He'd created the success he'd always wanted.

This year, his company, Justice Creek Barrels, had made number 245 on the Inc. 5000 list of America's fastest-growing companies. The broke nobody from the wrong side of town had officially arrived.

He had it all. Except Nell, who was stubborn, full of pride and unwilling to let go of the past and admit that they belonged together.

Didn't matter, though. She could keep on refusing him. He wouldn't give up.

And, one way or another, she would finally be his.

This, tonight, was a big step. She'd actually said yes to him, even if it was only for a drink. He had to go carefully with her, he reminded himself. If he got too eager, pushed too fast, she'd be off like a shot.

Still, as he led her to a quiet corner booth at the casino/hotel's most secluded bar, he had a really hard time suppressing a hot shout of triumph. Or at the very least, a fist pump or two.

She slid into the booth on one side and he took the other. The light overhead brought out the deep, gorgeous red of her hair. Her eyes, green as a secret jungle lagoon, watched him warily.

God, she was beautiful. Even more so than when she used to love him. And back then she'd been the most beautiful girl in the world. All the guys had wanted a chance with her.

But she'd only wanted him.

He'd thrown her away. Sometimes even a smart guy made really bad choices.

It had taken him eleven years and a failed marriage to face the truth that he was one of those guys. He didn't love easy, but when he finally did, that was it. *She* was it, the one for him. For four never-ending months now, he'd been actively pursuing her. In all that time, she'd never given so much as a fraction of an inch.

Until tonight.

Her mother had been right. He'd needed to get her away from Justice Creek and all the reminders of how bad he'd messed up with her back in the day. Vegas was the perfect place to finally get going on the rest of their lives together.

Now, if he could just keep from blowing this…

Nell tried to figure out where to begin with him as the waitress came, took their orders and returned with their drinks.

When the waitress left the table for the second time, Nell took a sip of her cosmo and jumped in. "Why me—and why won't you take a hint that I'm just not interested?"

He stared into his single malt, neat, as if the answer to her question waited in the smoky amber depths. "I don't believe you're not interested. You just don't trust me."

"Duh." She poured on the sarcasm and made a big show of tapping a finger against her chin. "Let me think. I wonder why?"

"How many times do I need to say that I messed up? I messed up twice. I'm so damn sorry and I need you to forgive me. You're the best thing that ever happened to me. And…" He shook his head. "Fine. I get it. I smashed your heart to tiny, bloody bits. How many ways can I say I was wrong?"

Okay. He was kind of getting to her. For a second there, she'd almost reached across the table and touched his clenched fist. She so had to watch herself. Gently she suggested, "How about this? I accept your apology. It was years ago and we need to move on."

He slanted her a sideways look, dark brows showing glints of auburn in the light from above. "Yeah?"

"Yeah."

"So then we can try again?"

Should she have known that would be his next question? Yeah, probably. "I didn't say that."

"I want another chance."

"Well, that's not happening."

"Yes, it is. And when it does, I'm not letting you go. This time it's going to be forever."

She almost grinned. Because that was another thing

about Deck. Not only did he have big arms, broad shoulders and a giant brain.

He was cocky. Very, very cocky.

And she was enjoying herself far too much. It really was a whole lot of fun to argue with him. It always had been. And the most fun of all was finally being the one in the position of power.

Back when they'd been together, he was the poor kid and she was a Bravo—one of the Bastard Bravos, as everybody had called her mother's children behind their backs. But a Bravo, nonetheless. Her dad had had lots of money and he'd taken care of his kids, whether he'd had them by his wife or by her mother, who was his mistress at the time. Nell always had the right clothes and a certain bold confidence that made her popular. She hadn't been happy at home by any stretch, but guys had wanted to go out with her and girls had kind of envied her.

And all she'd ever wanted was Deck. So, really, he'd had all the power then.

Now, for some reason she didn't really understand, he'd decided he just *had* to get another chance with her. Now, she was the one saying no. Payback was a bitch, all right. Not to mention downright delicious.

He finally took a slow sip of his Scotch. "Look. It almost killed me to lose you. But I couldn't afford you then. You have to know that. I had things to do, stuff to make happen." His eyes were brown in this light, brown and soft and so sincere. "I had nothing to give you then."

"I wanted nothing from you and *you* know that. Nothing but your love."

He looked away. She stared at the side view of his

Adam's apple. Just like old times. "Come on, Nellie. I had too much to prove. It would never have worked then."

He was probably right. "And it's not going to work now." She leaned across the table toward him, held his gaze steady on and concentrated on trying really hard to get through to him. "I don't trust you. I *can't* trust you. It's not that I hate you. I don't. I don't *despise* you. I just want you to let it go. Leave me be and move on."

He drank more Scotch. "Have dinner with me." She opened her mouth to say no, but then he reached out and covered her hand with his. The words backed up in her throat. "Just dinner." His grip was hot and a little bit rough, and it felt unbelievably right.

How could that be? Words and breaths and even her heart felt all tangled up together in the base of her throat, all tied in hot, sweet, hurtful knots. She opened her mouth to tell him no and he slid his thumb under her fingers, into the vulnerable secret center of her palm, and squeezed, just a little.

Impossibly, she squeezed back. The light from above caught in his eyes, burned in them.

She swallowed, hard. "It would…only be dinner."

The flame in his eyes leaped higher. Dear, sweet Lord, had she really said that? She needed to take it back this instant. She pulled free.

He didn't try to hold on, just slid his hand back to his side of the table and said in a neutral tone, "Only dinner. That's good."

And she couldn't help thinking that, really, what could it hurt? Here, in this glittery, sprawling desert city where nobody knew them? It could be a good way, a *graceful* way, to finally say goodbye.

* * *

He took her to the hotel's French restaurant, Quatre Trèfles. The food was wonderful and there were several courses, different wines offered with each new dish.

Nell drank sparingly. She planned a full day at the trade show tomorrow and didn't want to be hungover. Plus, she needed all her wits about her when dealing with the impossible man across the white-clothed table from her.

Deck looked so good by candlelight. It burnished his thick brown hair and brought out the wicked gleam in his eyes. She had to watch herself around him, she really did. She wanted to handle this goodbye evening with grace.

There was actual chitchat. He asked how she'd gotten into business with Garrett. She explained that after two years at Colorado State, she'd had enough of college. Garrett was doing pretty well building houses. She'd started out working for him. They got along well together.

She laughed. "He's always calling me a pain in his ass."

"But he couldn't get along without you."

"You've got that right. A few years back, he wanted to start building spec houses. I put in some of my inheritance for that and we became partners."

Deck talked about his barrel business, which he'd started eight years ago in the garage of the house he'd been living in then. At the time, he'd tended bar at Teddy's Bar on East Central Street. Essentially, Justice Creek Barrels found and sold whiskey and wine barrels to winemakers, breweries and distilleries. His company also made barrel furniture and other custom barrel-based gadgets and knickknacks. In the time he'd been building JC Barrels, he'd also managed to get a business degree, taking classes online and at State.

She asked about his sister, Marty. "I heard she got married."

"Yeah. His name's Hank Jackson. He's a good guy."

"I'm glad."

"They live in Colorado Springs. And as of three weeks ago, I'm an uncle."

"Wow." Nell remembered Deck's younger sister as too thin and painfully shy, one of those girls who seemed to want to be invisible. "A boy or a girl?"

"Little boy."

"Have you seen him?"

He nodded. "Hank called me when Marty went into labor. I drove straight to the hospital."

"You were there for the birth?" For some reason, the thought of him jumping in his big, black Lexus SUV and racing to be there for his nephew's birth did a number on her heartstrings.

"Well, I sat in the waiting room for four hours, until the baby was born. Eventually, they let me in to see them. Marty was exhausted, but she was smiling. And I got to hold the baby. They named him Henry, after Hank."

"Give Marty my best?"

"Sure."

"And, um, your dad?" Keith McGrath had been a major issue between them, when it all went to hell. Maybe she shouldn't have mentioned him, but avoiding the subject would have felt like cowardice on her part. Plus, the whole point of spending this evening with him was to let the past go.

"I don't see him often." Deck's voice lacked inflection. He sounded careful. Too careful. "But he's all right. He manages an apartment complex in Fort Collins, does a little carpentry on the side. He's, uh, been doing pretty well the past couple of years."

"Excellent." She allowed herself a small sip of wine.

Deck regarded her distantly for several uncomfortable seconds—and then he changed the subject, which was fine with her. Great, as a matter of fact. It was only an evening they were sharing, not the rest of their lives. Yes, she wanted to talk honestly, but they didn't need to get into anything too messy.

After dinner, they gambled a little.

And then, around ten, he suggested, "Take a walk outside with me?"

She wanted to, she really did. But it was too cold out and, really, she ought to just tell him good-night. "It's windy and in the forties out there and my jacket is upstairs."

"No problem. We'll go up, get our coats. You can put on some walking shoes if you want to."

She let him take her arm and lead her to the elevators.

They went up to her floor first. She let him in her room, because to make him wait in the hallway would have been as good as admitting she felt awkward being with him in a room with a bed. It only took a moment anyway, to change into flats and grab her coat.

They got back on the elevator. He had a suite on the penthouse floor. She stood in the living area and gazed out over the waterfall lagoon below and the lights of the strip farther out as he disappeared into the bedroom.

"What do you see down there?"

She turned and gave him a smile. "Bright lights." He'd thrown on a gorgeous leather jacket and she couldn't help remembering his hand-me-down shirts and beat-up Vans with the holes in them back when they were kids.

Down on the main floor, they went out the lobby entrance, under the porte cochere and around the famous waterfalls and the minilake out front. As they strolled under the palm trees, she buttoned up her coat against the wind.

And when he took her hand?

She let him. Because this was a real goodbye at last, and it felt good to be with him finally in this friendly, easy way. If touching him still thrilled her more than it should, well, so what?

She wouldn't act on that thrill. She was only enjoying a last, companionable evening with an old flame, making peace with the past, ending things gracefully.

At a little after midnight, he took her back to her room. He didn't try to kiss her at her door. Which was great. A kiss would be too intimate and she would have ducked away.

With a whispered "Goodbye, Deck," she went in and shut the door.

The next day, she half expected to find him waiting in the hallway outside her room when she went down for breakfast.

He wasn't. And she was *not* disappointed. Last night had been perfect. She'd had a great evening with him; however, it really was over between them and had been for eleven years. He must be on his way home by now.

After breakfast, she went to the trade show and spent the morning watching installation demonstrations and connecting with granite, marble, tile, concrete and quartz composite distributors. At around eleven, she met up with Sherry Tisbeau, who lived in Seattle and worked with her husband, Zach. Tisbeau Development built condos mostly. Nell had struck up a friendship with Sherry a few years back. They'd met in LA at Build Expo USA. This trip, Sherry had brought along Alice Bates, the Tisbeau office manager.

At half past noon, just as Sherry was suggesting they ought to go get some lunch, Nell spotted a guy who looked like Deck. He lounged against the wall by a granite dealer's booth about twenty feet away, a glossy brochure in front of his face. Her pulse started racing and her stomach got quivery.

As she gulped and stared, he lowered the brochure, revealing that gorgeous, dangerous slow smile. Every nerve in her body went on red alert. It felt amazing. Invigorating. And scary, too.

She knew she was in trouble and somehow didn't even care.

She turned to Sherry. "Listen. I see an old friend and I need to spend some time with him. I'm going to have to take a rain check on lunch."

Sherry gave her a hug and reminded her to keep in touch. A moment later, the two women were gone and Deck stood at her side.

She met those eyes and felt as light as a sunbeam,

fizzy as a just-opened bottle of Dom Pérignon. It had to stop. She needed to remind him that they'd said goodbye last night. And then she needed to leave. If she hurried she could catch up with Sherry and Alice.

About then, she noticed the lanyard around his neck and the official trade-show badge hanging from it.

"You stole someone's badge," she accused.

His grin only deepened, revealing that dimple on the left side of his mouth. "They wouldn't let me in here without one." Way back when, she used to watch for it, that dimple. She used to hope for it. It only appeared when he let himself relax. He rarely relaxed back then. He was constantly on guard.

How completely things had changed.

He took the badge between his fingers. "But then, luckily, I found this one on the floor outside—and it's not stealing if I found it on the floor."

Just turn and leave him standing here. Walk away and don't look back.

But she didn't budge. Instead, she opened her mouth and something stupid came out. "We're here in Vegas. Stuff happens in Vegas and that stuff is meaningless. That's all this is."

He gave her the lifted eyebrow. "Meaningless, you mean?"

"That's right. It's just for now. Nothing more. Nothing changes when we go home. I have my life, you have yours."

For way too many glorious seconds, they simply regarded each other. She had that sense she used to get with him, when they were together so long ago. The sense that they were the only two people on the planet.

Finally, he asked, "Hungry?"

She slipped her arm in his. It felt absolutely right there. "Starved."

She never returned to the convention floor.

They had lunch and then they played the slots. She had a great time.

Was she being an idiot?

Oh, absolutely. She knew she shouldn't give the guy an inch.

But he was so much fun—a lot more than he used be, now that'd he'd found the success he'd always craved. There was an easiness about him now, a confidence that made him even more attractive than before, if that was possible. She liked just being with him.

And why shouldn't she indulge herself? Just a little. Just for this short time that they were both here in Vegas.

She got lucky and won a thousand-dollar jackpot. She collected her winnings.

Then he suggested a couple's visit to the hotel spa, of all things. No way she was passing up an offer like that.

They took mud baths side by side and he told her all about the things you could make with a barrel, everything from cuff links to wall clocks, chandeliers to yard art. They got massages, their two tables pushed together. It was intimate in the most relaxing, luxurious sort of way. And she went ahead and allowed herself to love every minute of it.

After that, they had facials, then mani-pedis. Somehow, he looked manlier than ever, sitting in that pedicure chair as a sexy blonde took an emery board to his toes.

It was a little past six when he left her at the door to her room.

"I'll be back for you at seven thirty," he said in a tone that teased and warned simultaneously. "Be ready."

She was ready, all right. In her favorite short black dress, sleeveless and curve-hugging with a cutaway back, her red hair pinned up on one side by a rhinestone comb, wearing killer black heels with red soles. His eyes darkened when she opened the door to him, and his gaze moved down her body, stirring up sparks. He wore a gorgeous graphite suit and she wondered how she'd gotten here, about to spend an evening that could only be called romantic with the penniless, dark, damaged boy she used to love, the boy who'd grown up to run his own company and look completely at ease in the kind of suit you couldn't buy off a rack.

She grabbed her beaded clutch and her metallic Betsey Johnson wrap and off they went.

Down at the lobby entrance, beneath the porte cochere, he had a car waiting. She sat beside him on the plush leather seat and stared out the tinted side window as they rolled by one giant pleasure palace after another, the bright lights melting into each other, gold, green, red, purple, blue. Eventually, the driver turned down a side street and stopped in front of modest-looking restaurant with a red-and-white-striped awning over the door.

Inside, they sat beneath a stained glass ceiling with chandeliers shaped like stars. They had champagne and caviar, lobster bisque and the best filet mignon she'd ever tasted, the meat melting like butter on her tongue.

Okay, yeah. It was dangerous, doing this with him. Every moment she spent near him she could feel herself giving in to him, the sharp edges she used to protect herself leaving her, morphing into vulnerable softness that invited his touch.

He leaned across the table and so did she. She shouldn't have, but she was full of a happy, giddy sort of longing—to savor every minute, to get closer.

And closer.

And then he touched her, so lightly, a brush of his index finger across the back of her hand, over the bones of her wrist, up her forearm, drawing the nerves with him, making a trail of pleasured sensation along her skin. She shivered, a hot kind of shiver, the kind that promised forbidden delights to come.

"It really can't happen," she whispered.

"Why not?" That voice of his, sweet and rough, was like raw molasses pouring out.

She was in trouble. Worse, she was loving it. "A thousand reasons. It's over. You know it. It's been over for years."

"Nellie." His finger at her elbow, sliding higher, over the bright tattoo that covered the evidence of what he had been to her. "It doesn't feel over. *That's* what I know. And you know it, too, whatever lies you think you have to tell yourself."

She caught his hand, gently pushed it away. She sipped more champagne and treated her taste buds to another wonderful bite of buttery steak. "This is like some kind of dream. And I really need to wake up."

A moment later, he somehow had her hand in his.

He turned it over, smoothed open her fingers and pressed those warm, soft lips of his into the heart of her palm, his breath like a brand on her skin, his beard scruff tickling just a little. "Remember that first time?"

"Oh, God. In a tent." They'd been seventeen. It was the summer between their junior and senior years, and they'd hiked up into the National Forest, to Ice Castle Falls, pitching the patched-up tent he'd brought in the center of a clear spot, a miniature meadow not far from the falls.

She'd told her mother that she was going camping with a group of kids. Willow might have been Frank Bravo's accomplice in cheating on his wife Sondra for more than two decades, but when it came to her daughters, she had certain rules. No overnights with a boy as long as Nell was underage. So she'd lied and said she was sharing a tent with Shonda Hurly, a friend from school. Deck hadn't needed to make up stories about his plans. His father had a lot of stuff going on and pretty much let Deck do what he wanted.

Across the table, still holding her open palm in his hand, Deck said, "I couldn't believe I got so lucky, to spend a whole night with you."

"Too bad about the ants." She laughed and he laughed with her. And then the laughter faded. They watched each other across the table, the tender old memory fresh and new between them. They'd gotten down to their underwear before they realized they'd pitched the tent on an anthill. "I did a lot of shrieking, as I recall."

"They were all over you."

She'd slithered out of the tent, twisting and turning

in the moonlight in her white cotton panties and sports bra, madly slapping ants away. Deck had followed her out. He'd put his hands on her shoulders and told her to stand still. And she had. She'd stilled—for him. And he had run his hands all over her, starting with her hair, her neck, her shoulders and on down, until all the ants were gone and there was only his tender, wonderful touch.

Then he'd gathered her close to him, pressed his lips to her temple, her forehead, her mouth. She'd kissed him back, twining her arms around his neck, whispering of her love.

It was chilly up there in the mountains at night, even in summer. So they shook out their clothes and put them back on and moved the tent to the other side of the cleared space.

And then they'd crawled back inside, wrapped their arms around each other—and been each other's first time. She remembered it as awkward and intense. And beautiful, too.

Even later, after he'd stomped all over her heart, she couldn't quite bring herself to regret choosing him for her first.

The car was waiting out in front when they left the restaurant.

She felt so soft and pliant by then, her mind a happy haze from the champagne and the wonderful food, the sweet, shared memories—and Deck. Laughing with her. Touching her. Reminding her of just how good it used to be.

When he pulled her down across his lap, she let him. She kicked off her shoes, folded her legs on the seat and gazed up at his wonderful face as the bright lights flowed over him, turning his skin from gold to red to blue. He smelled of some dark spice, familiar in the deepest way. She could ride like this forever, her head in his lap, wrapped in the scent of him.

In no time, the car glided in beneath the porte co-chere at their hotel. She sat up, smoothed her hair and slipped her shoes back on.

Inside, he took her hand and she let him. He led her straight to the elevators. They went up. She made no objection when the car kept right on gliding upward past her floor.

At the door to his suite, she hesitated. "We're going to have to…" That was as far as she got, because his arms went around her.

"Listen," he said.

"What?"

And then he kissed her for the first time in over a decade.

She couldn't suppress the low, pleasured hum that escaped her as his lips met hers. He just felt so good. And, well, she wanted it, that kiss, wanted those strong arms around her. So she didn't push him away.

On the contrary, she pulled him closer, sliding her hands up that hard chest of his, up and over his thick shoulders to clasp around his big neck. He tasted of the cinnamon in the coffee they'd had after dinner— hot and wet and so very right.

Her wrap slithered to the rug at their feet and she hardly noticed it was gone.

He was…bigger. Broader. More encompassing than before. She'd known that already. After all, she had eyes. But there was something so much more immediate about *feeling* it, about having him hold her, surround her. His body gave off waves of heat. That hadn't changed. And he smelled even better than she remembered—of that unnameable, too-tempting spice and also faintly of some no doubt ridiculously expensive cologne.

"We have to talk," she blurted out anxiously when he finally lifted his head.

"That's a bad idea." His hands brushed up and down her arms and she knew he was soothing her, settling her to his will. The ploy should have annoyed her, *would* have annoyed her if only his touch didn't set her on fire.

How long had it been since she'd felt this way, like she might burst out of her skin with longing? Like if she didn't make love with this guy tonight, she just might crumple to the floor in a swoon of unsatisfied lust, of thwarted desire?

Too long. Forever. A lifetime, at least.

Not for eleven years, if she let herself be painfully honest about it. Deck just…did it for her in a big way.

No other guy even came close.

Not that she would ever tell *him* that.

Somehow, she made her lips form the words that had to be said first. "We need to set boundaries."

A couple of swear words escaped him.

She put the tips of her fingers to those wonderful lips. He stuck out his tongue and licked them. She almost gave it all up right then, grabbed him close again, kissed him hard and long, demanded he take her to his bed right this minute.

But no. Things had to be said. Though she shouldn't be doing this, right now her yearning exceeded her need for self-protection by an alarming degree. She just couldn't resist him tonight.

But they needed a clear agreement as to how it would be. "We talk first."

"Nellie—"

"We talk first or I'll say good-night."

"You can't go now."

"Watch me." She tried to step back.

He only held on. But at least her insistence had gotten through to him. He gave in to her demand with a reluctant nod. "All right. We'll talk."

Bending, he picked up her wrap and handed it to her. She took it gingerly, draping the filmy, glittery fabric over her arm as he turned away to run his key card past the reader. The green light flashed.

He pushed open the door.

Chapter Three

He led her into the sitting area. "Drink?"

"No, thanks." She set her wrap over the back of the sofa and smoothed it with nervous hands. Everything felt strange suddenly. She shouldn't be here.

There was no excuse for her to be here, to give in to him in this massive, impossible, stupid way.

He took off his suit jacket, tossed it over a chair and loosened his beautiful blue tie. His shirt was a gorgeous, lustrous light gray and his watch was a Blancpain. She knew because her father used to have one and she had wanted that watch so bad. She would have worn it proudly if he'd only left it to her. He hadn't. He'd left it to her half brother Darius, the oldest of the nine of them, which she'd eventually let herself admit was fair.

"What?" He gazed at her with equal parts desire and impatience.

She kept the sofa between them, resting her hands on the back of it. "I need your agreement that this isn't going anywhere, that it's just for now, for while we're here in Vegas."

He dropped into a big white chair. Spreading his knees wide, he rested his arms on the chair arms, like some barbarian king holding court. "How many times do we have to go over this?"

"Until I'm sure that you agree and understand my, er, terms."

"Your terms." He seemed to taste the words and to find them not the least to his liking. "We don't need terms. Just do what you think you have to do. I'll do the same."

She was suddenly absurdly glad for the fat sofa between them, as if it was any kind of real barrier, as if it could actually protect her from what she would do with him here tonight. "I just don't want you to get any ideas about how things could change when we go home. They won't. When we're home, I'm not getting near you. I'm going to pretend that tonight never happened." She waited, expecting some sort of response from him.

Sprawled back in the chair, he just stared at her. She felt her skin heating, her resolve weakening. It was absurd—*she* was absurd. But something had happened since last night, when she'd given in enough to have a drink and dinner with him. Something had happened as she'd spent the afternoon and evening with him today. She'd had the advantage before.

But that advantage was gone. She really ought to miss it more.

And still he said nothing.

Oldest tactic in the book: the one who speaks first loses.

She spoke. "Yeah, okay. I want you, Deck. I want you a lot. And I'm starting to get that this is something we just need to do. We need to get it out of our systems, find closure between us once and for all..."

Dear God. What was the matter with her, spouting all this tired psychobabble? Talking about "getting it out of our systems," like sex was a juice cleanse. And "finding closure," as though closure was something a person could misplace.

Those phrases were meaningless, really. Just the stuff people said when they were about to do something stupid.

And facing him now across the nonbarrier of the sofa, she knew absolutely that having a Vegas fling with Deck was a giant bowl of stupid with several spoonfuls of trouble sprinkled on top.

But she was going to do it anyway, whether she could get him to agree to her terms or not. She was going to do it because she couldn't bear not to. Because she was almost thirty and he was the only man she'd ever been in love with. Because one thing had not changed: when he touched her, it all felt perfectly, exactly right.

He said, "I want you, too, Nellie. I always have."

Bitterness rose in her. *Too bad that didn't stop you from throwing me away.*

Then he held out his hand to her. His eyes were soft and yearning, wanting her the way she wanted him.

And in the space of an instant, her bitterness turned achingly sweet. She couldn't scoot around that sofa and grab on to him fast enough.

His fingers closed around hers and he gave a tug, bringing her up flush between his spread knees. Already, he was hard for her, the ridge of his arousal obvious beneath his fly. The sight of it thrilled her, almost had her dropping to her knees to get closer, to make short work of his belt and his zipper, set him free to her eager touch, her hungry mouth.

He brought her hand to his lips, licked the bumps of her knuckles, causing havoc inside her, bringing up goose bumps along her arms. "I have a request."

"Yeah?" It came out on a hungry hitch of breath.

"Take everything off. I want to see all of you. I've waited so long…"

Breathless moments later, she stood before him wearing nothing but the rhinestone comb.

"Nellie," he said, low and dark and wonderfully rough. "You are more beautiful even than I remember. That shouldn't be possible. But you are." He commanded, "Bend down here."

She bent from the waist. It felt like heaven, to bend to him, to give in to him. For now, for tonight and tomorrow, she had no need to resist him. She would have this night and tomorrow. Then on Monday, she would go home and set about pretending that none of it had happened.

Did that make her a liar and a coward and a fool?

Absolutely.

Her hair brushed his cheek. He framed her face with his strong hands. "Kiss me."

She didn't have to be told twice. Their lips met in a kiss that burned her down to her core. His tongue came invading. She welcomed the tender assault on her senses. He made her belly quiver. Without even touching them, he made her nipples ache and tighten.

As he kissed her, he slid the comb from her hair and dropped it to the little table by the chair. Freed, the red waves fell around them. He speared his spread fingers up into the thick mass of it, rubbing it into her scalp as though bringing up a lather, then closing those big fingers into fists, pulling a little, drawing her mouth even closer, sealing their lips together hard and fast, dipping his tongue in deeper.

When he finally loosened his hold on her, she had to remind herself to breathe. Lifting away a little, she stared down him, dazed with want. He gazed back at her, pupils dilated, black holes she could get lost in, never to be found.

They were both breathing hard. She felt herself falling into him, wrapping herself in his heat and his hunger that so perfectly matched her own, vanishing into him, though neither of them had moved.

"You won't get away, Nellie," he whispered. "I won't blow it this time. You and me. That's how it's supposed to be."

"Don't go there." She made her voice as low and rough as his. "Or I am leaving."

They glared at each other, a battle of wills.

And then he gave her that slow, dangerous grin.

Suddenly, they were both laughing.

His hands clasped her waist and he came up out of the chair. She gasped at the speed of the move, canting back, making room for him—and let out a shriek of surprise as he boosted her high and laid her over his shoulder. "Deck!"

But he wasn't listening. He put his hand on her bare

bottom, spreading his fingers, holding her where he wanted her. "Steady. I've got you."

And then he was moving, headed for the open bedroom door.

He laid her down on the turned-back bed. "Don't you dare move."

She only chuckled, grinning up at him, bringing her arms up and sliding them under the pillow beneath her head.

His eyes blazed down at her and he muttered a string of dark, delicious promises—of what he would do to her, how much he wanted her, all the ways he was going to drive her wonderfully, totally insane. And then he got out of his clothes, tossing them every which way, over a shoulder, in the general direction of the bedside chair. He threw that fancy watch at the nightstand. It dropped to the carpet. He just left it there.

When he came down to her she grabbed him close, her mind and heart and body ready, so ready, to be with him. There was no past or future tonight.

There was only right now.

And then he was kissing her, a thousand kisses or maybe a million. He said he needed to put his mouth on every single inch of her body.

She indulged him that. Gleefully, eagerly, she braced her hands on his shoulders and pushed him lower, murmuring huskily, "Wait. I think you missed a spot. Oh! Yes. There…"

Was it as good as she'd imagined it might be in her forbidden, delicious fantasies?

Better. So much better.

There was time for teasing. And there was time for overwhelming, intense kisses, for his big fingers inside her, playing her so well that she shattered in the space between two ragged breaths.

And, after that, he only played her some more, adding his wonderful mouth to the equation, until she was crying out, clutching his head, begging him, "Please, please, Deck. Please make it now. Oh, yes. Like that..."

After the third time he carried her to the peak, tumbling over, she took charge, pushing him to his back, worshipping every hard, glorious inch of his body the way he'd done to hers. She traced the tendons and veins on those big arms of his, bit the hard, high bulge of his biceps, followed the crisp trail of hair across his broad chest.

And on down.

She wrapped both hands around him and lowered her mouth to him. Somehow, for a little while, he held his natural inclination to take control in check. She savored every second of having all the power, taking him deep, relaxing her throat.

Taking him deeper still.

In the end, he couldn't help himself. He had to take the lead, even in her pleasuring of him. He cradled her head between his big hands, holding her still for him.

She relaxed into it, letting him do what he wanted with her. It was glorious, so good. And at the last second he did let go, he let it happen, let himself go over. She looked up at him on his knees above her, his big head thrown back, a long, deep groan rolling from his throat.

She drank every drop of him. He tasted like the ocean, salty and rich.

Then he pulled her up to him, into his arms, settling her close to him in the tangle of sheets and blankets. He stroked her hair, traced the bumps of her spine, rested his broad hand in the naked curve of her waist.

Did she sleep for a little? It seemed she must have.

There were dreams, of the two of them, in the good times, years ago. Laughing together by a campfire, sharing a whole conversation in a glance across a classroom, walking the hallways at Justice Creek High, his arm across her shoulders, his body pressed just right along her side.

Invincible. That was how she'd felt with him. That as long as they were together, nothing could beat them. They ruled their private world of two.

He never knew what might happen at home. His father always had some big plan in the works that never seemed to pan out. Deck had never talked about it much, but Nell knew things hadn't been easy for him and Marty. The way Nell understood it, Keith McGrath loved his family, but he was just always distracted. He couldn't seem to get a job and hold on to it. The McGrath family struggled constantly just to get by.

Nell's issues weren't nearly so bad. But it was no fun, what went on in her family. When her dad's first wife died, he'd married her mother and moved Willow into the house he'd built for wife number one. Nell had still been living at home then, so she'd moved, too. It was awful, going home to the house that had belonged to her father's first wife, to her resentful half sister Elise and Elise's best friend, Tracy, who had been taken in by Elise's mom years before, when Tracy's parents died suddenly. Elise always acted so prissy and ladylike. However, being ladylike didn't stop her from coming up with new ways to torture Nell. It was a war in the Bravo mansion back in those days, a war in which Nell fought just as dirty as Elise.

But sometimes, even though you don't believe it could ever happen when life is crappy, things do get better. It had for Elise and Nell. Now, she and Elise were tight. They would do anything for each other. Too bad they didn't know back then how it would all work out.

It was the same with loving Deck, really. She'd been so happy with him in high school. Looking back, she was glad she hadn't known how it would turn out with him. She'd had no clue that he would shatter her poor heart and that it would take her forever to recover from losing him.

Like that ancient Garth Brooks song that her mother used to love, where life was a dance and if you'd known ahead of time how bad a loss was going to be, you might have just said no to whatever was destined to break your heart.

But if you said no to love, you would miss the dance.

And, really, now that she was over it, over *him*, she could let herself admit that the dance of their young love had been pretty damn spectacular.

She could honestly say now, at last, after all these years, that she wouldn't have missed loving Deck for the world.

As for this brief, thoroughly magical reunion they

were sharing? No way would she have wanted to miss this, either.

She tipped her head back to look at him.

His eyes were open, watching, waiting.

She offered her mouth and he took it.

The magic began again.

And when he got the condom from the bedside drawer, she took it from him, rolling it down over him. He rose above her, his eyes gleaming almost golden in the light from the lamp.

He came into her and she took him, deep and true. She wrapped her whole body around him and they moved together, in perfect rhythm, all the way to the top of the world and over into free fall.

She called his name, among other things. She had no idea what crazy words came out of her mouth as her body pulsed around him.

All she knew was that it was perfect, this moment. This last dance together with the boy she'd once loved beyond all reason.

He wasn't that boy anymore. And she was no longer the girl who had given her heart and trusted him not to break it.

Which was fine. As it should be.

And this, tonight, was just what she'd needed, a Las Vegas fling with the grown-up Deck McGrath.

In the gray light of the next morning, he reached for her. She melted into him. They made love, sweet and slow.

After the loving, they ordered room service. They had breakfast in bed and then made love again. They took a long bath. Together.

And made love again.

More than half the day had passed and all they'd done was eat breakfast and take a bath—oh, and the lovemaking. Lots and lots of lovemaking. She was dizzy with it, swept away into a beautiful, sensual dream, a private fantasy, a lush, secret world containing just the two of them.

By late afternoon, he let her go down to her room. But only long enough to shower, put on a little makeup and get dressed. He was at her door a half an hour after she'd left his suite.

He started kissing her. No surprise where that led.

Finally, they both agreed they needed to get out, have some dinner. The big bed would be right there waiting for them when they returned.

She put her dress back on. He ordered a car and off they went to an Italian place he knew about. The food was wonderful and there was a really nice Chianti. Maybe she had a little more of that than she should have.

They got back in the limo.

Deck shut the privacy screen between them and the driver. They glided up and down the strip, making love. Even through the tinted windows, the bright lights reached them and played a symphony of color across their naked skin.

There was champagne. Dom Pérignon.

"When did you order champagne?" she asked, sitting there naked, feeling satisfied, shimmery all over, somehow. It was really quite wonderful.

He said, "You are so beautiful, Sparky. Bold and strong and so damn smart. More than any man deserves in this life. There is no one, *no one*, like you."

His words poured over her. They made her feel special. Treasured. Loved.

He never did answer about the champagne, not that she really cared. He popped the cork and gently pushed her down onto the seat so he could pour the bubbly treat on her belly. He sipped it from her navel. She wove her fingers in his hair and sighed in delight.

He said more thrilling things, lots of them, whispering them against her bare skin—that he loved her, that she was and always had been the only woman for him.

She took what he said as part of the fantasy he was weaving around her. No, they weren't real, his vows of love and forever. She didn't believe them.

But they sure sounded good. They went down just right with the champagne, with the feel of his hot, hard body pressing close, with the endless pleasure he gave.

It was paradise, pure and simple, to be held in his arms.

When the limo slowed and glided to a stop, she opened her eyes and asked, "Where are we?"

He chuckled. "Put your dress back on. We'll go check it out."

"An adventure?" That sounded delightful.

"That's right. Nell and Deck's big adventure." He helped her back into her clothes. Once she was dressed again, she sat there grinning like a fool as he put on his shirt, his boxer briefs and his pants. She wasn't really drunk, just…kind of high. High on pure pleasure, on sexual satisfaction.

He was fully dressed now. He held up her coat and she put it on.

Dazed, happy, glowing all over, she let him help her from the car.

They were at the Clark County Marriage License Bureau, of all things. That made her laugh. "Oh, you are kidding me."

He took her hand. "Come on, let's go inside, just for fun."

"But…it's nine o'clock on Sunday night."

"Sparky, this is Vegas. They almost never close." He gazed down at her expectantly.

She thought about how much she was loving this, every minute of this night, the two of them together, kind of hazy from the alcohol, loose and easy all over from the beautiful lovemaking. What a great way to feel. She was ready for anything.

"All right," she said. "Let's go inside."

She followed him in.

After that, well, whatever he suggested, she couldn't say yes fast enough. She let him take a number and when their turn came, she whipped out her driver's license and signed where the clerk pointed. It was all very simple. Smooth and easy as you please.

When they returned to the limo, they had a marriage license.

Really, why was she doing this? She wasn't that drunk. She didn't understand herself. She ought to…

But then he started kissing her again. And it was a game they were playing. Delicious. Thrilling. In a way, the whole thing was like a dream, *her* dream, from so long ago, the dream that didn't come true.

Somehow, impossibly, it was coming true tonight.

It wasn't that far to the wedding chapel—well, it was more of a wedding complex, really, a series of pink stucco buildings and a parking lot dotted with palm trees and spiky succulents. The limo slid to a stop and Deck pulled a small velvet box from his pocket.

Inside was a gorgeous ring. He slipped it on her finger, a perfect fit, and she thought, *He's got this all planned.*

That should have alarmed her, right?

Definitely.

But the ring was so beautiful, with a large square-cut diamond, smaller diamonds glittering along the platinum band. And everything just felt…right somehow. Tonight, she was living the teenage fantasy she'd once believed in so passionately—the fantasy of her and Deck and happily-ever-after.

The years between then and now had somehow folded in on themselves. He'd never taken a buzz saw to her heart, never married someone else.

Her life with him, the love he'd always promised her. Their own personal forever…

It was coming true at last.

The chapel complex had it all, everything two people needed to say "I do," Vegas style.

The woman in the lobby area greeted Deck by name. "Mr. McGrath." She practically cooed at him. "Welcome to Now and Forever." She aimed a thousand-watt smile at Nell. "And it's a delight to meet your beautiful bride." The woman took Deck's black credit card and sent him to the men's boutique to rent a tux.

Another woman came for Nell. "I'm Anita. And I'm so glad you've come to us for your special night. Follow me."

In the bride's boutique, Nell chose her dress. It was perfect, that dress, with a low back and lace sleeves—a mermaid dress, clinging to her body all the way to her knees and then opening out in a fishtail of lace and glittering beads. A seamstress quickly pinned and tucked at the waist and down over her hips, creating a perfect fit. And then she whisked the dress away to alter it on the spot.

Nell chose shoes with rhinestone bows and open toes. The dress had a built-in bra, but Anita offered an adorable pair of lacy satin tap pants that would look so sexy when the dress came off. Nell said yes.

She put on the pretty tap pants and the perfect shoes. As Anita helped her into the altered dress, a clear thought came swimming up through the sensual haze created by thrilling lovemaking, good champagne and a long-held secret fantasy at last coming true.

She really ought to pay her share—after all, she'd always been a girl who carried her own weight. "I want to pay for my part of this," she instructed Anita.

Anita laughed. "Oh, no. That will never do. Mr. McGrath was very clear that he will be taking care of everything."

"But I—"

"Let a man feel like a man," Anita suggested in a coaxing whisper, as if Nell would be doing Deck a favor to let him run up a giant bill.

Nell wanted to argue. But to argue would kind of ruin the fantasy, wouldn't it?

She let it go. If he wanted to spend his money, who was she to put the brakes on? "Fair enough, then."

"Excellent." Anita beamed. "Personal items—the shoes and the lingerie—are only for purchase. The dress, though, is up to you. It's offered for rental. But if you love it, Mr. McGrath said to tell you it's yours."

Mr. McGrath. She knew he must be eating this up, the poor boy who half the time didn't know where his next meal would come from, grown into a man who could whip out his credit card and buy out some Vegas wedding boutique.

She stared at her reflection in the full-length mirror. Oh, she did love the dress. "It seems kind of extravagant…"

"Honey, it's your wedding dress." Anita knelt to adjust the frothy fishtail hem. "It's a once-in-a-lifetime thing and if you love the dress, you should have it."

Nell smiled at her reflection, a smile that trembled only a little. "Well, all right then. I'm going to keep it."

"That's the spirit." Anita had her veil ready. It was full-length. Because, hey, might as well live this fantasy for all it was worth. Anita pinned it in place with a rhinestone band.

Nell decided on a bouquet of red roses and white lilies, all festive and Christmassy. Why not? It would be Christmas soon. She chose a red rose and red Christmas berries for Deck's boutonniere. Another saleslady appeared and rushed off to take it to him.

Anita settled Nell's veil over her face and led her to the Gardenia Chapel, where the starkly simple altar had tall silver candlesticks on either side and a silver wall behind it, a wall draped in a shining curtain of crystal beads. The wedding march played, and Nell walked down the aisle to where Deck, in a tux, stood with the pastor, waiting for her, his bride.

She knew a moment's stark panic. Really, what was she doing here in this silver chapel dressed as a bride?

But Deck was waiting. And she wanted to be with him. Her heart settled into a happier rhythm and, slowly, her eyes on him through the white film of her veil, she went to him. He watched her come, his mouth curved in that dangerous smile, his eyes full of equal parts heat and tenderness.

Anita was right there to hold her bouquet. Deck took her hands and they said their wedding vows. Of course he had a wedding ring for her, a thick band with diamonds in a braided pattern. He slipped it into place next to her spectacular engagement diamond.

Finally, reverently, he lifted her veil and kissed her. She sighed against his parted lips, deep in this wedding dream, together with her only love.

At last.

They signed more papers. Deck would receive their marriage certificate in the mail within ten days. She started to ask why it wasn't going to her place.

Then again, what did it matter really? Deck could handle logistics. He'd certainly done a great job of it so far. Right now was magic time, and thinking too hard about anything just seemed like a bad idea.

A photographer appeared to take pictures. She kissed Deck again for the camera and wished that this perfect fantasy might never end.

He had more champagne waiting in the limo. She had a glass, just to keep the fizzy, happy feeling going.

Back at his suite at the hotel, he helped her out of her wedding finery. They made love for hours.

Finally, he pulled her in close and traced the tattoo hidden among the dragonflies and flowers on her left arm: his name.

She'd been just seventeen when she'd had it written on her skin, *Declan*, in the symbol for infinity. She'd gone all the way to Denver to do it and used a fake ID. Because she loved him and he loved her and their love was forever.

Until it wasn't.

After the second time he dumped her, she'd had it camouflaged with a half-sleeve of ink because she couldn't stand to look at it anymore. The tattoo artist she went to that time had been a genius. She'd woven Deck's name into a complex, brightly colored design. Now his name looked like just part of the filigree pattern in a dragonfly's wing. Nobody could see it.

Except Deck. He knew where to look. He always had.

Deck pulled up the covers. She snuggled into the shelter of his cradling arms, closed her eyes and let herself drift off to sleep.

When she woke, there was a sliver of gray daylight showing between the drawn curtains.

Morning already. She felt a moment's regret. Today she had to go home.

Deck slept beside her, his eyes closed, his face easy in slumber. She watched him for a moment, her heart welling with something a lot like happiness. When she turned her head to check the clock, she saw it was ten after eight.

She felt…satisfied. Every inch of her body well-used. A little sore, maybe, but in a good way. She was also a bit hungover from the champagne, but not too bad.

Her flight would take off at 11:15 a.m. She should get up, go back to her room, have a shower, get her things together.

But something was bothering her, a sense of dread

kind of pushing at the corners of her consciousness. She stared up at the ceiling, starting to frown.

There was definitely something…

Something she'd done that she probably shouldn't have.

Something…

Wait a minute.

Images from the night before flashed through her mind.

The Italian place. She'd had a little too much Chianti, hadn't she? And then, in the limo, sailing along the strip, making love. Drinking champagne.

But the champagne was no excuse. She hadn't been *that* drunk. She'd been perfectly cognizant of everything that occurred.

She'd *let* it happen, been nothing short of complicit in what had gone down.

When, out of nowhere, they'd stopped at the place to get a marriage license, what had she done? Followed him in like a lamb to the slaughter.

And when he'd whipped the ring out of his pocket, had she said, "Declan Keallach McGrath, you hold on just a minute here? What is that ring doing in your pocket? What do you think you're trying to pull? No way am I falling for this crazy scheme"?

No, she had not.

She had said nothing.

Nothing at all.

Instead, she'd let him take her hand and slip that ring on her finger. And then she'd clung to him like a happy little barnacle to the hull of a ship, offering her mouth up to him, kissing him like she would never get enough of him as they rolled on down the strip to that wedding place called Now and Forever.

Now and Forever...

Oh. My. God.

The mermaid wedding dress. The flowers. The Gardenia Chapel. The ring...

The one he'd had ready and waiting in his pocket.

Reluctantly, already knowing what she would find, already feeling the unbelievable truth wrapped around her finger, she pushed back the covers enough to raise her left hand to eye level.

Diamonds. Sparkling furiously at her.

Sweet Lord in heaven.

What had she done?

Chapter Four

A long string of crude words escaped her. She muttered them in a low, angry whisper.

And Deck? He remained sound asleep, looking perfectly relaxed and not the least bit guilty, though he had seduced her in the worst kind of way.

Seduced her into marriage. The dirty, rotten creep.

How dare he lie there peacefully sleeping at a time like this?

"Deck!" She grabbed his giant shoulder and shoved at it, hard. "Wake up, Deck. Now!"

He made grumbly, sleepy noises and opened one eye. "Nellie. Sweetheart." He smiled at her drowsily. "C'mere." He reached for her.

Oh, no way.

She kicked free of the covers and leaped from the bed. "Keep your hands to yourself."

He gave her that killer smile and a long, slow, hungry look.

She realized she was naked. "Don't you *even* look at me like that." Snatching up her pillow, she pressed it to her torso, smashing it close with both arms. It wasn't much, but at least it covered the crucial bits. "We need to talk."

"Talk?"

"What? Is there an echo in here? You heard what I said."

He sat up, the sheet falling away from his broad, lightly furred chest and corrugated abs. Lazy and unconcerned, he stretched and yawned. She clutched her pillow tighter and waited for him to stop showing off all those muscles as if nothing was wrong.

"Okay," he said finally, shoving his own pillow behind him, leaning back against it and lacing his hands on his head. "What's the problem?"

"What's the problem?" she shrieked.

He let his hands drop. "You're shouting."

She made herself speak more quietly. "Everything, Deck. It's *all* the problem," she insisted in a low, angry growl. "We agreed on a Las Vegas fling. We agreed that it would be over and done by the time we went home, that *when* we went home, you would stop chasing after me, that you would go your way and leave me to go mine. We *agreed*. You said you were fine with it."

He looked at her tenderly. *Tenderly*, damn it. "Think back, Nellie. I was never fine with it."

"But you *agreed* to it."

He answered so quietly. "No."

"Yes." She held on to her temper by a very thin

thread. "You agreed and I trusted you and all that time you were busy planning our...wedding? Who does that? Who *thinks* like that? How can you keep insisting that it wasn't the way it actually was?" She held up her ring finger and shook it at him good and hard. "Never in a hundred thousand years did we ever agree to *this*."

"Now, Sparky..."

"Uh-uh. Don't you do that. You don't get to call me Sparky at a time like this."

"Can you just look at things reasonably, please?"

"Oh, cute." Her blood felt like it was literally boiling. "Now you're lecturing me about being reasonable. After what you did."

"Come on. Get honest. You were there. You signed the license, you put on my ring, chose your dress and decided on the flowers. You walked down the aisle to me and you said, 'I do.' It's not like I drugged you and married you against your will."

Okay, fine. He was right. Kind of.

Except that he wasn't. Except that he'd planned it. He'd played her so well.

She raked her sleep-scrambled hair back off her forehead and launched into a fresh attack. "Oh, yes, it *is* like you drugged me. You know that it is. You followed me here to Vegas and you turned on the charm. And when I couldn't resist you, you said you understood that it was only a fling—or if you didn't actually *say* it, you sure did imply the hell out of it. Then you lulled me with champagne and loved me all up and down the strip and then you took me to that chapel and I...well, I..." Her fury devolved into sputters. *Because there is no excuse for my own behavior.*

That was the real problem. That was what made her the maddest of all. She *had* gone along with it, relished every moment of it. She'd been complicit in everything they did.

Her fury redoubled. In sheer frustration, she raised her pillow and bopped him a good one on his big, stubborn head. When he only blinked and stared at her, she hit him again.

"Hey! Cut it out." He snatched it away from her, leaving her standing there naked *and* empty-handed.

She let out a low moan of total exasperation and wrapped her arms around herself. "This is so wrong. I have no words for how wrong this is, Deck."

"Listen." He stuck her pillow behind him, too. "I know you're scared. But you don't have to be. Because it's going to be all right—better than all right." His eyes were all melty, all tender and hopeful. "We'll work it out, you'll see. Nellie, you know in your heart that this is what we both want. This is what we should have done all those years ago. Because you were right about us and I get it now. I had to go more than a decade without you. I even married the wrong woman. She knew I didn't love her the way that I should. She knew there was someone else. And that someone else was you—always, Nellie. You. I want a family, with you. Because we're *it* for each other, made for each other. We *need* to be married. We need to go home and start working on our life together."

She didn't know what to feel. Her damn, stupid heart ached to believe him, that she was his only one, that he only wanted her and only ever had. That it really could work, the two of them together now, when it had ended so painfully all those years ago.

She ached for…all of it. For him. And for her. Even for his ex-wife, disappointed in her marriage and in her love. She longed to ask him to tell her more.

But it just wasn't right, what he'd done, what had happened. This was no way to make a marriage, and they needed to face that. "It's not the end of the world." She made her voice even and reasonable this time. "I can put off my flight home and we'll pull ourselves together, get dressed and go find a lawyer, or whatever. We'll get a quickie divorce and that will be that."

"But, Sparky," Deck replied so very gently, "I can't do that."

"What do you mean, you can't? There's no *can't*. Just say yes and let's go."

"Uh-uh. I mean it. I can't."

"Why not?"

"Two reasons. One, I love you. And two, I don't want a divorce."

She face-palmed at that one. And then she fisted her hands at her sides and groaned at the ceiling. "All of a sudden, you *love* me."

He just sat there, looking infuriatingly droolworthy with his bed-messy hair and his scruffy, square jaw, his broad, muscled chest and that mouth that could kiss her like no other mouth ever had. He just sat there and said, "I've always loved you."

She had nothing to hit him with. Damn it. "Well." She spoke through clenched teeth. "And didn't you have some really painful ways of showing it."

"Nell. Come on." He reached out a hand. She ducked back from his touch. "Settle down. Let's discuss this reasonably, like two grown adults."

"Apparently, you haven't been listening to what I've

been saying. I'm not discussing jack with you. But I do have a question."

"Anything. Just ask."

She flashed her ring finger at him again. "How long have you had these?"

"Nellie…"

"Just answer the question, please."

He coughed into his hand. "A few months."

A human volcano, that's what she felt like. A human volcano about to blow. "You planned this whole thing, didn't you? You had it all arranged. At Now and Forever, they knew we were coming."

"If you would only take a few deep breaths and—"

"No, Deck. Just no."

"I don't want a divorce."

"You said that. I heard you. But that's just too bad, isn't it? Because *I* do want a divorce. And you don't get to be married to me if I don't want to be married to you."

"Well, now, wait a minute. I think you're kind of wrong there."

"Oh, really? How's that?"

"Because we *are* married. And before I even consider a divorce, I want you to give me—give *us*—a little time to see if we can make it work."

"I cannot even begin to express to you all the ways that is *not* going to happen." She cast a quick glance around the room, looking for her clothes—not the rhinestone shoes, sexy tap pants and white mermaid gown thrown in an explosion of beads and lace across the bedside chair. Uh-uh. The others. She needed the dress, shoes and underwear she'd had on when they left the hotel last night. When she didn't see them, she marched around the end of the bed and headed for the door to the sitting room.

"Where are you going?" he asked her bare retreating backside.

She just kept moving right on through the open door.

Her dress and underwear were in a wad on the sofa, her shoes beneath the coffee table. She grabbed her panties, put them on, wiggled into the bra and pulled the wrinkled dress over her head, reaching back, catching the zipper and managing to tug it closed without too much trouble. She was straightening the skirt when he appeared in the doorway to the bedroom.

Still naked. Still everything she'd ever wanted in a man. Except for the awful way he'd hurt her in the past. And the heedless, overbearing way he'd manipulated her last night.

"Talk to me, Nellie," he said in that gentle tone that made her want to break things—preferably over his big, fat head.

She put on her shoes. "Forget it." She grabbed her purse. "I want a divorce."

"Look. Just…don't go. Let's talk this out." He looked so sincere. It made the ache inside her intensify all over again.

But they weren't getting anywhere and he was far too tempting—not to mention overwhelming.

Space. She needed some of that and she needed it right now.

She took off his beautiful, perfect diamond rings,

set them carefully on the coffee table and stood tall to face him. "Admit it. You tricked me."

"Sparky…"

"Uh-uh. Just no. I'm going home. I can't deal with you now. At this moment, I only want to kill you in a thousand gruesome, painful ways."

"I didn't know what else to do, how to get through to you. Every time I made a move, you would cut me right off. I've tried, tried for years, to forget you, to move on. But it's just not happening. And you can lie to me all you want, Nellie. But we both know it's the same for you." He looked at her directly, without pretense, standing there naked and unashamed in the doorway.

The thing was, she believed him. And she *had* been complicit. No matter how skillfully he'd seduced her into it, when the preacher asked the big question, she had willingly, joyfully even, said, "I do." And yeah, he had it right about her. She'd never really gotten over him. No other guy compared.

Which meant that if she stayed, who knew what she might let him talk her into next?

She had to…protect herself. She had to get away, think, decide what *she* wanted to do.

Last night, he'd sapped her will and her good sense. Not to mention somehow miraculously gotten her to forget her pride and her absolute determination never to let him rule her again.

The man had told her what she wanted and seduced her into agreeing with him.

Yeah. Seduction. That's what this was. A seduction that had lasted the whole weekend. It had started with a drink and dinner on Friday night, and culminated in a diamond ring, a white dress and a walk down the aisle.

He'd taken her over.

Well, he wasn't taking her over today. Uh-uh.

She snatched up her tiny, jeweled purse and walked out the door.

Chapter Five

Hours later, Nell pulled her F-150 XLT pickup into her covered parking space in the lot behind McKellan's Pub on Marmot Drive in Justice Creek.

Ryan McKellan, who owned the bar and had the loft next to hers, came out the rear door and went around to the hatch at the rear of the camper shell to meet her. She popped the latch and he hauled out her bags for her.

"Good trip?" Rye asked, as she shut the hatch and locked the doors.

"Words fail me."

Rye was a longtime friend and knew her well. "Bad?" He held out his arms.

She stepped into the hug gratefully. "I'll say this much. It's good to be home."

When he let her go, he asked, "Whatever it is, we're

here and we're ready to listen." *We* meant Rye and his fiancée, Meg Cartwell, who tended the bar in McKellan's and shared his loft with him. The two were getting married in mid-December.

"Thanks. I may hold you to it. Right now, though, I need to get my stuff upstairs and call Ma."

"Calling your mother the minute you get home. That can't be good."

"You have no idea."

An hour later, Nell marched up the wide front steps of the Bravo mansion and between the ostentatious white pillars. It was a week and a half before Thanksgiving and there was already a giant Christmas wreath on the front door.

Her mother must have warned Estrella Watson that Nell was coming. The longtime housekeeper pulled the door open before Nell got a chance to knock. "Nell! Welcome." Estrella was a complete sweetheart. She'd been running the mansion for almost forty years, since way back when Frank Bravo built it for his first wife, Sondra. That Estrella got along so well with Willow Bravo was a mystery to everyone in the family. "How have you been?" she asked.

"It's a very long story and you really don't need to hear it," Nell grumbled, and then added more warmly, "Always good to see you, Estrella."

"Come in, come in. Your mother's expecting you." Estrella ushered her into the grand entry hall, which was already decked from floor to vaulted ceiling in greenery, lights and shiny glass ornaments. Nell shed her coat and Estrella took it from her.

"Everything's looking seriously festive around here."

"I know it's strange to decorate for Christmas before it's even Thanksgiving, but your mother said it was all right, so I got an early start this year." The housekeeper's expression turned wistful. "I love getting the house ready for the holidays and I just couldn't wait to do it up right one more time." Estrella had given her notice months ago and would retire in January.

Willow was remarrying in December—the Saturday after Rye and Meg—and moving to Southern California with her groom, Griffin Masters. She'd signed the mansion and its contents over to Nell's half siblings, Sondra's children, which only seemed right and fair to everyone, given that Frank Bravo had built the mansion for Sondra.

Still, Willow's generous gesture had taken both the siblings and half siblings by surprise. *Generous* and *fair* had not been words anyone would have used to describe anything Willow did—up till now.

"Darling." Willow appeared in the doorway to the front sitting room. She wore a white cashmere sweater and perfectly tailored wool pants, her blond hair short and shining around her still-beautiful, heart-shaped face. "Isn't this a lovely surprise? I'm so glad I was home when you called."

"Ma."

"Don't scowl so, Nellie. You'll get frown lines. Nice trip to Vegas?" Did she look smug? Willow had no shame, whether she was stealing Sondra Bravo's husband—or manipulating her children. "Come on into the library. I'll mix you a martini."

After what had happened the night before, the last thing Nell wanted was a drink. "I'll take coffee."

"I'll bring it right in," said Estrella.

"To the library, my love." With a sweep of one slender hand, Willow gestured Nell ahead of her.

They went through the sitting room to the library beyond. In addition to the glass-fronted built-in bookcases that lined the walls, there was a lit-up tree in the corner and a fire in the ornate, greenery-bedecked fireplace.

Nell took a seat on one of the two damask sofas in the center of the room as Willow, at the fancy glass-topped drink cart, whipped up a martini. "Is Griffin here?" She would just as soon not yell at Willow in front of her fiancé if that could possibly be avoided— not that she *would* yell.

Uh-uh. She was not letting her temper run away with her, no matter how crazy Willow made her.

Her mother granted her a radiant smile. "Griff is off at that shop of Carter's." Carter was the oldest of Nell's four full siblings. He built custom cars for a living. "Carter's customizing a Bentley for him, of all things. You know men and their cars. He'll be back by dinnertime." Gently, Willow stirred her drink, then put on the strainer and strained it into an antique crystal cocktail glass. She speared an olive on a toothpick and lovingly dipped it into the glass.

Estrella appeared with the coffee. She set down the tray on the coffee table in front of Nell and bustled off.

Willow sat in a wing chair and enjoyed a slow sip of her drink. "Delicious. Now, tell me all about your trip to Sin City. Some trade show, as I recall?"

Nell took her time pouring coffee from the silver service, adding cream and one cube of sugar. "You know why I'm here, Ma. Don't play innocent. It's just not you. Deck admitted you're the one who told him where to find me."

Another delicate sip from the beautiful stemmed glass. "I happen to like Declan. More important, *you* like him—you *more* than like him. You're smart and strong and loving, my darling. But you're also prideful and stubborn and slow to forgive. I just wanted to give you a little nudge, that's all."

"Stay out of my life, Ma."

"Look at it this way. Soon I'll be living in California. You won't have to worry about me interfering in your life. If you choose to throw away what you long for the most, well, at least I won't have to be here to watch you doing it."

Nell reminded herself again that she would not, under any circumstances, lose her temper. "You know that I don't want anything to do with him."

"Darling. Stop lying. He's the one for you and the sooner you stop pretending he's not, the happier both of you will be."

Nell stared down at her untouched coffee and shook her head. "Why did I come here? What was the point? You know that telling him where to find me was wrong, but you did it, anyway."

"And I would do it again." Willow raised her martini high. "To love. And happiness." Another tiny sip. "Now. Tell me how it went. I'm guessing it was glorious. Just you and the man you've always loved, alone together in Las Vegas."

Denials rose to her lips. She bit them back. They would only make her sound defensive, give her mother more chances to call her a liar. "How about this, Ma? *You* tell *me* that you're sorry."

"Why? We both know I'm not."

"But you should be. Because you were wrong to tell him where I was."

"I don't care if I was wrong. Sometimes we have to do wrong to make things right."

"Even your platitudes are twisted, you know that?"

"Yes, well. We all know that I've never let other people's ideas of right and wrong determine how I live my life. I do what I need to do. Yes, I have been wrong, *terribly* so. I realize that. But this—my telling Declan where to find you? That wasn't wrong. That was creating an opportunity. For you and for the man who loves you to finally reach out to each other. It was your chance to begin to heal a wound that's been festering for much too long, keeping you both from the happiness you so richly deserve." Turquoise eyes glittering, she set down her drink, crossed her legs and leaned in. "Now, confess. You spent some time with him, didn't you?"

"I'm not telling you anything about my private business. Not ever again."

Willow just smiled. "Meaning you *did* spend some time with him and he's starting to get through to you."

"I never said that."

"Darling, you didn't have to. It's written all over your beautiful face."

Mondays were usually a little slow at McKellan's. As a rule, Ryan and Meg took Monday nights off.

Meg, who had wildly curling light brown hair, a lush figure and the kind of smile that could light up a room, knocked on Nell's door at a little after seven. "Hungry? I made lasagna."

"I'm in." She followed Rye's fiancé to the other loft, accepted ice water in lieu of wine and sat down to Caesar salad, plenty of hot garlic bread and Meg's amazing four-cheese lasagna.

"So what happened in Vegas?" Rye asked.

Nell must have made a face because Meg chided, "Rye. Maybe she doesn't want to get into it."

Rye reached over and gave Nell's shoulder a squeeze. "Come on. You can tell us. We'll keep your secrets."

Nell realized she really did want to talk about it with someone she could trust. "I'm not ready to tell the family yet." Which was silly, and she knew it. Her sisters could be counted on to keep her secrets to themselves.

But she'd grown extra close to Meg and Rye the past couple of months. Maybe it was being next-door neighbors. Or maybe it was Meg, who had that bartender's talent for listening and accepting, for saying the right thing just when a girl needed to hear it.

Meg said, "Only if you want to tell us. Nobody's putting you on the spot."

"Speak for yourself." Rye made a silly face at Meg and she swatted at him. They were so cute together, Nell could hardly stand it.

Somehow, that kind of did it, watching Rye and Meg being happy together. Somehow, that made up her mind for her. "Ma told Deck where to find me in Vegas."

Rye groaned in her behalf. "And he showed up there?"

"What do you think?"

Rye grunted. "He showed up."

"Yes, he did. I was really mad at first, but then, I

went ahead and agreed to have a drink with him. And then we had dinner and then, well…"

"Wow." Rye put down his fork and sat back in his chair. "You had a thing with Deck in Vegas?"

"It was more than a thing."

Meg reached over and clasped her arm, a steadying, comforting sort of gesture.

Rye asked gingerly, "More? In what way?"

And she just went ahead and said it. "I married him last night."

The silence at that table was absolutely deafening. Finally Rye asked, "But…why? How?"

So she told them. Everything—well, not all the naughty bits, but the basics. That they'd spent Saturday and Sunday nights together and on Sunday night, he'd taken her to a chapel, where she'd walked down the aisle to him.

Meg went ahead and stated the obvious. "But…he's not here with you now."

"I had a fight with him this morning."

Rye asked, "A fight over…?"

"He planned the whole thing. He set me up and I fell for it. Saturday night, we agreed on a final fling, agreed it would be over as soon as we left Las Vegas. But then *last* night, when we got married, he had the rings already—he'd had them for months, he admitted to me this morning. We went to the chapel supposedly on the fly, but they were expecting him. And then this morning, when I put it all together, realized he'd totally tricked me and demanded an immediate divorce, he said no. He said not until we at least try to make it work. So I walked out on him. I came home." For some reason, she felt almost ashamed to admit that.

Meg asked in a near whisper, "Has he called? Tried to get in touch with you?"

"I have no idea. I turned off my phone."

Meg asked so softly, "Do you want him to try to reach you?"

"Oh, God." She put her hands over her eyes, as though by hiding her face she could hide from the awful truth. "Yes," she confessed, dropping her hands and staring miserably down at them. "Damn it to hell. Yes. For months I just wanted him to leave me alone. But…slowly, he's been doing it, reeling me in. And now, well, I can't help myself. I don't want him to stop."

Nell stayed with her friends until around eleven. They offered hugs and reassurances—that she was not alone, that people got suddenly married in Vegas all the time.

They promised her it would all work out and advised her to give herself time to think about what she really wanted and what her next step should be. When she left, they reminded her that they were there for her whenever she needed them.

At her place, she turned on the phone. Deck had left two voice mails.

One that afternoon: "Pick up the phone, Sparky. We have to talk about this—damn it, Nell. Come *on*."

And one just a couple of hours ago: "I'm not giving up. We're going to work this out. Call me. Now."

She almost called him back, but stopped herself in mid-dial.

* * *

The next morning, as she was catching up on paperwork at Bravo Construction, she heard his voice in the outer office.

"I'm here to see Nell," he said, bold as only he could be. "She's expecting me."

Her assistant, Ruby, knew the drill. "Sorry, Deck. You know it's not happening—wait! You can't... Stop!"

But he was Deck and he didn't stop. Her door swung open and there he was, looking altogether too doable in jeans, a white shirt and a gray tweed blazer that emphasized his big shoulders and narrow waist.

Ruby called from behind him, "I tried!"

"Thanks, Ruby, I'll deal with it."

He stepped in and shut the door.

She closed the lid on her laptop so that she could glare at him unobstructed. "You're in my place of business. I did not invite you here and I want you to go."

He flipped back the sides of the blazer and braced his hands on his hips. "When will you talk to me?"

"Soon."

"When is soon? I need a date, a time and a place."

"Not now. You just said it. Time and place, Deck. This is neither."

"When?" The guy just wouldn't give up.

Her heart raced, her breath came hard and her pulse fluttered madly in her throat. She wanted to kill him— or else grab him and kiss him and beg him to swear to her that everything would be all right. "I need a week."

He turned around, stalked to the window and then stalked right back. "A week from today."

"That's what I said. Next Tuesday. My place. Seven p.m. Until then, will you please just leave me alone?"

His eyes burned through her for an endless count of ten. And then, finally, he muttered, "You got it." He strode to the door and yanked it open. "See you then."

And he was gone.

After rising to shut the door again, she returned to her desk and called her half brother James at Calder and Bravo, Attorneys-at-Law.

At two that afternoon, James's secretary ushered Nell into his office.

James got up for a hug, then he offered her one of the guest chairs. She took it and he settled in behind his desk. He said his wife, Addie, was doing just great and his adorable one-year-old stepdaughter was growing like a weed.

Then James asked, "So what can I help you with?"

She felt suddenly wary, though James was a good guy and totally trustworthy. "It's a legal thing. I need to know you can keep it confidential. It's…a little embarrassing and I don't feel like getting into it with the family."

James nodded, his blue eyes sincere. "I understand your concern. And as your lawyer, I will always observe strict confidentiality. Whatever you tell me, it won't leave this room."

So she told him that she'd married Deck in Vegas on the spur of the moment. "It was a mistake. And now I want a divorce."

James asked, "Are you sure?"

Okay, maybe she wasn't. But she had to do something, make a move. Take a stand. "Yes."

"How does Declan feel about it?"

"He says no—or he has up till now, anyway. He says he wants us at least to try to make it work."

James explained that he would get the paperwork together for her and help her fill it out. "Then I'll file your divorce petition with the court and arrange to have Declan served."

It sounded so complicated. "We've only been married for two days. Does it have to be a big deal? I don't want anything from him. Can't I just…fill the thing out and give it to him?"

"It's best to have a process server handle it. You are, however, allowed to mail his copy to him with a paper he can fill out and send to the court—but that's only going to work if the two of you are in agreement about ending the marriage. You just told me *he* wants to work it out."

"But *I* don't. It was a mistake, okay? He has to realize that and accept it. Doesn't he?" She felt like an idiot as she asked the question. Deck had been chasing her for months. And so far he'd shown no indication that he would give up—especially not now that he'd managed to lure her to the altar.

James looked at her patiently. "If you think he might contest the divorce or drag his feet or try to make things difficult, you really need to have him served. You need a legal record *that* he's been served. Then it will be his turn to respond, to accept or reject your terms, to add his own."

"You make it sound like it could drag on forever."

"Unfortunately, that does happen sometimes."

"It's all so…" She sought the word and sighed when it came to her. "It's sad, James. Sad and complex."

"Divorce tends to be that way."

She stood up.

He gave her a gentle smile. "I'm getting the feeling you want to think about it some more?"

"Yeah. I guess I do."

Deck wasn't at all happy about the way things were working out with Nell—or, more specifically, *not* working out.

At least he had a company to run, something to help him keep his mind off the infuriating woman he'd always loved, who swore she didn't want to be married to him.

Deck kept good and busy all day. He found five hundred rum barrels in the Dominican Republic, barrels that he already had standing orders for. Rum barrels were the hot thing for craft brewers, who wanted their beers to have complexity. Rum barrels gave specialty beers the wild, funky flavors craft-beer makers loved.

He had a long meeting with his CFO and another with the shop manager. Then he caught up with the sales team.

At six, he called it a day and went to Prime Sports and Fitness across Central Street from McKellan's. The gym was owned and run by Nell's brother Quinn. Deck spent a half hour on the elliptical and then worked out with weights, keeping watch the whole time for Nell, who had a membership, too. She never showed.

He saw Quinn, though. Nell's brother offered to spot him on his bench press. Quinn seemed the same as always—calm, quiet and helpful. If he knew that

Deck had married his sister night before last, he didn't let on.

The next day, Deck bumped into Clara Ames, Nell's half sister, on Central Street. Clara stopped to chat for a minute. She wanted to order some barrel wine racks for the restaurant she owned. They agreed she would come in to see him Thursday afternoon. As she waved and walked away, he was almost positive Nell hadn't told her what had happened in Vegas. The next day, when she ordered a dozen barrel wine racks and never said a word about Nell, or even so much as looked at him funny, he was certain she had no idea that he and Nell were married.

Saturday, he stopped in at Bravo Catering and Bakery for coffee and a blueberry muffin. Elise Walsh, Nell's other half sister, owned the place. That morning, Elise was working the register. She seemed the same as always, friendly but not overly so. He would bet she didn't know about him and Nell, either.

He couldn't resist wandering over to the flower shop, Bloom, next door, which Nell's sister Jody owned. Jody greeted him warmly. He bought a giant bouquet containing what looked like every flower known to man and then he suggested, "How about you send these to Nell?"

Jody laughed. "Nice try." He'd had Jody send Nell flowers one time, four months before. Nell had told her sister not to let him do that again.

He left the flower shop grinning. His guess? Nell hadn't told anyone in her family that she'd married him in Vegas.

Should that bother him? Probably.

But he couldn't help thinking that he might use the information to his advantage.

A better man would do no such thing.

But he'd never claimed to be any kind of saint. His mother had always been frail and unhappy. Lurline McGrath didn't have a lot of time for him or his sister. She was either sick or working herself into an early grave trying to pay back his father's debts. She'd died when he was eleven and Marty was eight, leaving them at the mercy of dear old Dad, who wasn't a bad man, just an irresponsible one. Keith McGrath always had a big plan to get rich—and inevitably ended up empty-handed and in debt to whoever he'd borrowed from last.

Deck had grown up determined *not* to end up like his father. He'd fought hard to make it on his own terms *and* always paid back what he owed. He was no saint, though. Sometimes he played it a little bit shady in order to get what he wanted.

And now that he'd finally gotten Nell all the way to the altar, he wasn't letting her get away without a fight. Yeah, he'd manipulated her to get her to marry him. But no way would she have said "I do" if deep down she didn't want what he wanted.

He only needed to find a way to convince her that she didn't really want a divorce. He needed time with her, damn it. And if he had to threaten to tell her secrets to her sisters to get that time, he would do it.

At JC Barrels, he gave the flowers to his top sales rep, Eden. Eden put them in a vase made of barrel staves and set them on a barrel table near the front door.

Then he called Garrett Bravo, Nell's partner at

Bravo Construction. They had a nice, long talk about the progress of the house Bravo Construction was building for him. By the end of that call, Deck was absolutely certain that Nell's brother had no clue she had married him in Vegas.

That night, he almost went to McKellan's. He liked it there. They had the best local beer on tap and the burgers were great. But Nell might be there. After all, she lived upstairs. She wouldn't like it if she ran into him. And he didn't want to do anything that might make her change her mind about their meeting Tuesday evening.

Somehow, he got through Saturday night. And Sunday. And Monday.

And then it was Tuesday at last.

When he knocked on her door, she pulled it open so fast he knew she'd been waiting on the other side. She wore yoga pants and a giant black sweatshirt with In Memory of When I Cared printed on the front. There were shadows beneath her jewel-green eyes, and she was just close enough when she pulled back the door that the well-remembered scent of her came to him, clean and tempting at once.

"You want something?" she asked. "Coffee? A beer?"

Just you. "I'm good."

The living area was all one space, ultramodern, with a contemporary gas fireplace, a sofa, coffee table and armchairs near the tall windows that looked toward the mountains to the west. She gestured in the general direction of the sleek, low couch. "Have a seat."

He went where she pointed.

She took the chair across from him, drew her stocking feet up and tucked them to the side. "I was thinking that I would have the divorce papers here and ready for you."

If he tried to kiss her, would she punch him? "I don't want a divorce, Nellie."

She made a halfhearted attempt at an eye roll. "You have made that unbearably clear." And then she sighed. "I went to see my brother James at his law office. He explained how a divorce is a lot more complicated than just filling out some forms and handing them to you. Long story short, I told him I would need to think about it some more."

Deck kept his expression noncommittal, but disappointment dragged on him. She'd actually seen a lawyer about a divorce. Also, the lawyer she'd gone to was James, her half brother. Who else had she told? Threatening to out their marriage to her family wouldn't do him much good if everyone already knew. "I take it you've told your family that we got married?"

She shook her head. "Just James. He's sworn to secrecy, because I went to see him as my lawyer. And Rye and Meg, I told them. But they promised to keep it to themselves."

Did that mean he could put his evil plan back in play? "So then, you really *don't* want your family to know."

She narrowed her eyes at him. "You're up to something. I can smell it. Just tell me. What are you doing, Deck?"

He surprised himself and came right out with it. "I was thinking that unless you agree to my terms, I would maybe threaten to tell everyone that you married me last weekend."

She groaned. "Dear God. You're going in for emotional blackmail now? What is the matter with you?"

"I never claimed to be perfect. And I want to stay married to you. I'll do whatever's necessary to make that happen. I think I've made that pretty clear."

"So your big plan is if I don't do this your way, you're going to bust me as a total idiot to my family?"

"I didn't say that."

"But it's what you meant—and you know what?" She threw up both hands. "Do it. You tell them. Tell my sisters and my brothers and my totally annoying matchmaking mother that we're married. See how that goes over when *I* admit that, yeah, I screwed up, drank too much champagne and ended up saying 'I do' with you in Vegas. See how that works out for you when I go on to explain that I don't *want* to be married to you and as soon as you wake up and smell the Starbucks, we're getting divorced."

This really was not going the way that he'd imagined it. He tried coaxingly, "There was a time when you begged to be married to me."

"Please. I was eighteen and madly in love. What did I know? I went home every night to the house my mother stole from Sondra. My half sister was waiting there to torture me, taking scissors to my favorite clothes, putting black hair dye in my shampoo. You were my true love, the best thing that ever happened to me, the one who finally understood me, the guy who would stick by me forever, the one who made everything right. Or so I thought until you kicked me to the curb twice. So, yeah, before you ruined everything between us I wanted to marry you and I made no secret of it."

For about the hundredth time, he tried to make her see it from his point of view. "We weren't even out of high school. I was flat broke. You were a Bravo. I couldn't come up to that, okay?"

"I told you not to worry about money. I told you I would take care of you."

"Nellie. By now, at least, you have to know me better than that."

She fiddled with a loose thread on one of her socks, looking anywhere but at him. "I hurt your pride." Her voice was softer now. "I get it. It's what you said the other night in Vegas. You had things to prove." She sent him a sideways glance. "And then I went behind your back and loaned your dad that money."

Good old Keith. He knew a chicken ripe for plucking when he saw one. He'd talked her out of five thousand dollars, said he needed it right away to keep a roof over their heads—and it should be just between the two of them because Deck was too proud to borrow money and didn't need to know. Nell had kept that secret from him for weeks. And then finally, she'd broken down and confessed everything. She'd cried and begged him not to be mad at her, because she only wanted to help. He'd realized right then that he had to call a halt with her. She just didn't get it, didn't understand how completely she'd stepped over the line. She just couldn't see that all he felt was shame when she told him—shame, like sharp, bloody teeth, gnawing away at his self-respect.

Now, so many years later, he watched her shift in her chair, lowering her legs and then drawing them up again on the other side. Now, all he wanted was to get closer to her.

But how the hell to make that happen?

He said, "All giving him that money did was make it impossible for me to stay with you."

"I didn't care about the money."

"But, Nellie, *I* did. I couldn't see then that you were only trying to help. All I saw was that it couldn't work with us, that no way was I getting married to a rich girl before I'd made it on my own—a rich girl I owed money to."

"It wasn't your debt."

"Yeah, it was. You gave him that money for my sake."

She folded her hands, looked down at them and then back up at him. Her soft lips trembled slightly. He wanted to comfort her, but he knew she'd only push him away. She said, "So you dumped me."

He nodded. "Even though it practically killed me to do it."

"Oh, and that's supposed to somehow make what you did to me okay?"

"I didn't say that. What I'm saying is that you weren't the only one hurt by what happened."

"Can you just not confuse the issue, please? *You* dumped *me.* *You* made that choice. If it hurt you to do it, well, how is that in any way my fault?"

"I didn't say it was your fault."

"Great. So stop making excuses for yourself. You dumped me. And then you turned right around and dumped me again…"

It was only the truth. He couldn't deny it. He'd walked away from her in the spring of their senior year.

And when she'd come after him again that summer, he ached so bad from the loss of her, he took her for a ride in his rattletrap pickup—so they could talk.

There'd been no talking. He drove out to a deserted spot where they used to go to be alone. He'd barely turned the engine off before they were all over each other.

It was so wrong that he did that, made love to her when he knew he wouldn't stay.

It had been raining when he started kissing her, a sudden summer thunderstorm, the raindrops beating at the roof and the windshield, making a hollow, empty, furious sort of sound.

Afterward, Nell had pulled on her cutoffs and zipped them up. She'd straightened her bra and tugged her shirt back down. And then she'd glanced his way at exactly the moment he was sliding her a guilty look.

Their eyes met and held.

That did it. She *knew*. She got it. What had just happened was only a moment of weakness for him, not the fresh start she'd been begging him for.

That time, there was no begging. That time, she got mad. *You dirty, rotten bastard. How could you?*

He'd said all the stuff a guy says when it's over— that it wasn't going to work, that he was really sorry and he would take her home.

She'd called him worse things than a rotten bastard then. *Forget it*, she'd screamed at him. *I don't need you to drive me. I don't need you for anything, not ever again. I'm out of here.* And she'd shoved open her door and jumped out. She was drenched to the skin in the space of a minute.

He'd reached across the seat to roll down the hand-crank passenger window. *Come on, Nellie. Don't do this. Get back in the damn truck.*

But she only stood there, the rain pouring down her face, sheeting over her hair. And she'd yelled in the window at him, *Go, damn you, Declan! Just go!*

He couldn't just go. He couldn't be with her anymore, but he had to make sure she was safe, at least. So he had sat there and waited for her to stop acting crazy and get in the pickup again.

She didn't budge, just took out her phone, turned her back to him and made a call. And then she'd started walking, trudging through the mud, hunched against the downpour.

He'd followed her out to the two-lane highway, where he drove at a snail's pace along the shoulder behind her, waiting for her to finally give up and let him take her home.

But she didn't give up. Not Nell. She just slogged along, never pausing, never once looking back.

He'd known for certain then. This really was the end. She wouldn't be coming after him again. He'd lost her forever this time.

Which was good, he'd told himself. It was right. It was what he needed, for her to leave him. Because it couldn't work with them. They were worlds and worlds apart.

Finally her brother Carter had appeared out of the rain in a souped-up canary yellow Plymouth Roadrunner. Nell got in the car and Carter hit the gas.

Deck didn't ease the pickup out into traffic again until the yellow car had disappeared around the next curve.

Two years later, he'd sent her a check, with interest, for the money his father had "borrowed." Nell had cashed the check and that was that—they were done.

Or so Deck had told himself at the time.

But then, well, the years went by. And he never really got over her. There was no one else who could even compare to her. Now and then he would see her—on the street, in a store. Always from a distance. Both of them took great care not to get close.

He always felt that tug of yearning just at the sight of her shining red hair, at the confident set of her shoulders, the sweet upward tilt of her chin. Not that he ever planned to do a damn thing about it. He knew she'd never let him near her again.

Six years after that day in the pickup, he and Kristy Brice started going out. A year later, they moved in together and a year after that, they were married.

Bad idea. Kristy tried her best to make the marriage work, but no woman wants to be a man's second choice. A year after they got married, Kristy said she knew he didn't love her and she was through being second best, that he'd always kept some part of himself separate from her and that he'd said another woman's name in his sleep more than once. When he wouldn't talk about it with her, Kristy went to her friends. They'd told her the old stories about him and Nell.

Then Kristy came at him with what she'd learned from her girls. "You still love Nell Bravo," she accused.

Hearing his wife say it right out loud like that had finally done the trick. Kristy had shocked him into realizing it was true.

He'd never really let Nell go. Not in the deepest part of himself.

Kristy divorced him. He felt regret that he'd hurt her, that he'd failed her as a husband. He'd gotten it all wrong, he knew that. It took him another year and a half to admit to himself that he not only still loved Nell, he wanted her back—that he would do whatever he had to do to make her give him one more chance. He really was trying to fix what he'd broken.

Unfortunately, Nell refused to get with the program. "It's too late, Deck."

"No. It's not."

"You have to let it go."

He really was losing her all over again. It was all going down for the third time. He'd never get this close again and he couldn't lose her now. He had to do something to stop the end from happening.

But what?

An idea came to him—half-baked, a little weak, but what else did he have?

He went with it. "Give me till Christmas. If you don't feel differently by then, if you still think it can't ever work, I'll see my lawyer on December twenty-sixth. I'll make it happen fast. You'll get served by the first week after New Year's."

"Uh-uh. No. You won't change my mind—not in a month, not ever." As she spoke, she drew herself up in the chair and lifted her chin high. Her mouth trembled slightly, though. Did that mean it was all false bravado?

Or was that only wishful thinking on his part?

Didn't matter. He was not giving up. "Just until Christmas. Give me—give *us*—that much of a chance."

Nell couldn't afford to be tempted by his proposition. It was a bad idea to indulge him in any way. She'd messed up big in Vegas. Now she needed to hold the line with him. "How can I ever trust you to do what you say you will?"

"I swear it, Nellie. If you still want a divorce on the day after Christmas, you've got it."

She was weakening and she knew it.

And, really, how *could* she? Hadn't he hurt her enough before? How could she even consider giving him another chance to stomp on her heart? "This is all wrong."

"No, it's not."

"It didn't work when we were kids and it's not going to work now."

"Damn it, Nellie." He stood up so fast she had to swallow a gasp. And then he came out from behind the barrier of the coffee table. She braced as he came closer. "A chance, that's all. I just want a chance with you. I know I messed up all those years ago. I know I hurt you—and then I turned right around and did it again. But, Nellie, I had nothing and it seemed to me that you had it all. I needed to prove that I could make it on my own, without anyone's help. I just… No way was I going to end up doing to you what my dad did to my mom, no way could I be the loser you married who ruined your life. I loved you and I wanted you, but it wasn't enough. I knew that I would only drag you down. So, yeah, I walked away from you. I'm sorry, so sorry. But, Nellie, I have paid. Because I lost you and you were what mattered most."

She stared up at him as he loomed above her. He had his hands stuffed in his pockets and his eyes were full of longing. And pain, too.

It hurt so bad to see *him* hurting. She could barely

keep herself in that chair. She wanted to reach up to him, gather him close, shower him with soothing kisses, promise him it was all going to be okay.

She ached to comfort him—because she still cared. She still cared way too much.

The inescapable truth came clear to her, finally.

If she really was done with him, she wouldn't be here right now. If she'd really had enough of him, no amount of good champagne and hot, sexy loving would have had her walking down the aisle to him.

Nell stared up at the man who had chased her relentlessly for months now, the man she'd sworn for years she would never so much as speak to again—and faced the truth at last.

She wanted another chance, too.

Chapter Six

Deck said, "Okay. I admit it. I don't have the first clue how to give you the love you deserve. I'm pushy and I want things my way and I'm not always as patient as I probably ought to be. Maybe if we'd stayed together for all these years, I would have learned by now. I'm bad at love, I know that. But I do want to learn, Nellie. I want to learn with you."

Her heart kind of twisted. Really, did he think *she* could somehow teach *him*? Did she know any more about this love-and-forever thing than he did?

Maybe not.

But she certainly hadn't found love and forever *without* him.

And she wanted that. Wanted forever with the right man. Could that really be Deck?

Her fast-beating heart seemed to think so.

Yeah, she did fear that the third time around with him would *not* be the charm. But she was going there, anyway. She'd tried running away from her feelings for him. Tried it for years.

And yet, here she was, married to him. Staring up at the face that still haunted her dreams, daring to hope that maybe this time they would make it work.

"Sparky," he whispered prayerfully. "Say you'll give me—give *us*—this last chance."

She gulped hard. And nodded.

His gaze flared hot. "Was that a yes?"

Her heart seemed to have lodged hard in her throat. She managed a desperate little whimper of sound and nodded again.

He looked down at her like he could eat her right up. "Yeah?"

And, finally, the words came. "We'll, um, give it till Christmas to see if there's any hope that this marriage might work. But I want you to—"

"Come here." He reached down, clasped her wrist and hauled her up from the chair.

"Deck, wait, I…"

Of course he didn't wait. Instead, he stole the words from her lips by wrapping her tight in his powerful arms and slamming his mouth down on hers.

She gave it up. Her conditions could wait. It felt too good, the taste of his mouth, his body hard against her, the scent of him, clean with a hint of spice, filling her head. "Deck…"

"More." He breathed the demand against her parted lips.

She kissed him back, kissed him slow and sweet and achingly deep. Kissed him *more*.

But then he started tugging on her sweatshirt. "I want this off you."

"Wait."

"Uh-uh."

She pushed her shirt back down and then pressed her hands to his chest. "Not so fast."

His eyes were a smoky gray now, full of sexy promises she couldn't wait for him to keep. "You just said yes. We have to celebrate. Where's your bed, damn it?"

"First, you need to hear me out."

He muttered something low and grumpy followed by a gruff "What, then?"

"First of all, we're going to be married. *Really* married. And that means we're going to be together, *live* together."

"Works for me." He tried to grab her close again.

She kept her arms braced on his chest. "Here. At my place."

He scowled and looked around. "It's nice," he finally said grudgingly.

"And yet somehow you don't look happy about the idea of living here."

"Because we should live at my house. Yeah, it's a rental until my new house is finished. But it's great. You'll love it. It's bigger than this and there's land around it. We can hike up into the forest, visit Ice Castle Falls just like old times."

"We can stay here and still go hiking."

"McKellan's is open till two. What about the noise?"

"Oh, please. I ran the build on this loft. The sound-proofing is state-of-the-art—and don't think I don't know what you're doing. It's called control and you have to have it."

He only shrugged. "Letting other people run things is way overrated." With that, he scooped her up in his arms, turned around until he had his back to her chair and then dropped into it, taking her down with him.

Again, he tried to kiss her, but she didn't allow it. She managed to slip her fingers between his lips and hers. "We'll compromise and spend weekends at your place."

"Agreed—can I have my kiss now?"

"There's more."

"Kiss me first." His lips brushed her fingertips.

With a sigh, she let her hand drop and offered her mouth to him. He took it. For a sweet, endless moment, she surrendered to the pleasure he brought, let herself revel in the wet glide of his clever tongue, in the taste of him, hot and just a little bit minty, in the sheer deliciousness of simply being held by him.

Then she pushed at his chest again. "And we *are* telling my family."

That caught him by surprise. "You mean my evil plan to threaten you with telling all never even had a chance?"

"Not a prayer. I've been keeping what happened in Vegas to myself for a week now and I don't want to do that anymore. It just creates…distance, you know? Distance from the people I care about. If we're doing this, we are putting it all right out there—that you followed me to Vegas and I couldn't resist you."

He gave her a lazy grin. "Well, I can't say I mind the sound of that."

"Good. Because I plan to confess everything, that

I gave in to your killer charm and married you in a gorgeous silver wedding chapel. We're going to tell them the truth and then deal with any possible family fallout up front and honestly. None of it will be a secret. Not even the fact that it might not last past Christmas." She bent close for another kiss.

He caught her face between his hands. The playful, happy light had left his eyes. "Slow down."

She couldn't resist taunting him. Just a little. "Not a fan of telling it like it is?"

"I'm all for honesty."

"Yet you don't look too happy about telling everyone the simple truth."

"I just mean we don't have go crazy on this whole honesty thing."

"Well, *I* meant what I said. If we're doing it, we're owning it."

He spent several seconds glaring at her before his hard look softened. "Full disclosure. You sure, Nellie?" He stroked a finger down her cheek and along the side of her throat.

She sighed in pleasure at the simple touch. "Full disclosure, absolutely. And did I mention there will be endless holiday family events? They're pretty much constant from Thanksgiving to New Year's around here. Including two weddings—my mother's to Griff, and Rye and Meg's. As my husband, you will be expected to go with me to all of them."

"Yes." He said it with feeling. "I give in. Anything, Nell. However you want it."

"And there's your sister, too." She laid her palm against his cheek, felt his heat and the pleasant prickle of his beard scruff. "I want us to drive to Colorado

Springs, to visit her and her husband, bring some gifts for the baby."

"You got it."

"And, Deck, we need to talk about your dad."

The light left his eyes and his face turned blank. "What about him?"

"We need to get together with him. We need to tell him we're married and working on making the marriage a forever thing."

"That's completely unnecessary."

"He's your dad."

"I don't want you having anything to do with him."

"He's your *dad*."

"You keep saying that."

"Because it's true. I'm not just pretending he doesn't exist. Plus, you need to know that you can trust me around him, that I'm not going to be taken in by him again."

"I already know that."

"Great. Then we'll go visit him. Together. Or he can come here."

Now he wouldn't look at her. "You're being unreasonable."

She slid off his lap and stood staring down at him, wondering how she was going to get through to him. "Deck…"

He looked up at her then. "It's not your damn call, Nell. *You* make choices about *your* family and *I'll* decide about *mine*."

"But you keep track of him, don't you, and you see him now and again?"

"So?"

"I'm guessing you help him out when he gets in trouble?"

"You were always way too damn smart, you know that?"

"So that's a yes, then? You do keep an eye on him and you do help him out now and then."

"Because I'm a controlling SOB and we *both* know that. For some reason I don't understand and refuse to examine deeply, I feel responsible for him, for the messes he gets into and the people he screws over. I send him money to help him get by because it's the right thing to do—and because maybe the money I send will mean one less poor fool he takes advantage of. But that's it. I don't see him all that often and I don't want you around him."

She wanted to give in. But that just felt wrong to her, like they would be leaving a big barrier between them, a scary question from the past, still unanswered. "We're grown-ups now. He can't hurt us. He only has power over us if we give it to him."

"Pretty words." He got up and walked around her to the island that marked off the kitchen area. When he faced her again, he had one word for her. "No."

Should she give it up? She really wished she could make him understand. "Your dad was…a big thing… between us. He's why you left me, Deck—okay, maybe not all of it. But he was the final straw. A very big final straw."

"That's in the past."

"And that's why I want us to go see him together. I want us to have a new memory of dealing with him, one where we are together, united, one where we can be kind to him and include him, while, at the same time, there's no way he can touch what we have."

Deck gripped the counter behind him and leaned back against the island. The muscles of his broad chest and shoulders popped into sharp relief as they stretched the fabric of his knit shirt. "I don't need a new memory of dealing with my father."

"But I do."

He looked down at his boots and then slanted his glance up to her again. "Give it up, Nellie. I agreed to all of your other conditions. Just not this one. Let this one go."

"I don't know if I can."

His square jaw hardened. "So the deal's off if I won't take you to the old man?"

She didn't want it to be off. Now that she'd said yes, she had hope, burning like a bright flame inside her. She wanted to see if just maybe they had a future together, after all. She wanted that a lot. "Will you at least think about it? Please?"

"Nellie…" His rough, low voice raised a pleasured shiver down the backs of her knees, sent a buzz of need vibrating along her spine.

She tried again. "Think about it."

"Is it a deal breaker?"

"Do you have to have all the answers right this minute?"

He watched her from across the open space, his gaze dark, calculating. Then he asked again, "Is it a deal breaker?"

"If you just have to know now, then yes. I want us to see your dad together. Please."

The silence stretched between them. He refused

to give in on the subject of his dad and she had made her point. There was nothing more to say about it right now.

Finally, he pushed off the counter and stalked toward her, his hot gaze never leaving her face. She hardly knew what she felt—relief, frustration, growing desire?

When he stood before her again, she could feel the heat of him.

All the other emotions faded to gray. There was only desire—vivid, immediate. Only the pull between them, the wonder of wanting him so very much, of knowing that when he touched her, she would be all his.

Again. At last.

"Give me your hand, Sparky." She held it out. A slow grin tugged the corner of his mouth and that dimple appeared, the one that told her he felt good, easy in this moment. "Not that hand."

She giggled like some silly kid and gave him her left hand. He dug in a pocket and came up with diamonds. "You brought my rings." He slipped them both on her ring finger. They looked so beautiful. She couldn't help smiling dreamily down at them. "I do love them. I…kind of missed them."

He raised her fingers to his lips and kissed the tips of them, one by one. "Good. I have your dress and your shoes and those sexy satin shorts, too."

She glanced up into his waiting eyes. "It was extravagant of me to ask for that dress. It's not something I'll ever have a chance to wear again."

"Maybe in forty years, when we renew our vows?"

She laughed. "That is not the kind of dress I'm going to wear when I'm seventy."

"Or maybe our daughter will wear it for *her* wedding."

Could they really be those people—the ones with children who grew up and had weddings of their own? The ones who were still together as senior citizens? She put her hand on his chest, felt his heartbeat, strong and steady, beneath her palm. "I want this to work, Deck. I honestly do."

"It *will* work." He bent closer.

She lifted her face to him. The night to come shimmered in the air between them—*all* the nights. A lifetime of nights, she fervently hoped.

As his mouth covered hers, he scooped her high in his arms.

In her bedroom, he took a strip of condoms from his pocket before tossing his jeans to a chair.

She said, "I'm on the pill."

"Yeah?" The dimple appeared in the corner of his mouth and his eyes gleamed blue-green in the light from the bedside lamp.

"Yeah."

He volunteered, "I've always used condoms and, except for you and me in Las Vegas, I haven't been with anyone since the last time I was tested. It always came back negative."

"Me, too. On all counts."

He tossed the condoms over his shoulder. She whipped back the covers and he grabbed her around her waist, taking her down to the sheets with him.

They tumbled together, laughing and kissing, peeling off the last of their clothing.

The kisses got longer, deeper, wetter, the hunger building, the heat flaring higher.

She was on fire for him, so crazy, so eager. No one had ever felt the way he did in her arms, so big and hard and exactly right. The rightness mattered the most. The way he could thrill her and still make her feel that sense of belonging, of coming home. She wrapped her legs around him and he came into her, filling her in a hard, hot glide, pushing deeper still.

Surging up to meet him, she moaned way too loudly at the sheer glory of it. His name was the only word she knew and she chanted it, "Deck, Deck, Deck," over and over, until the sound of it felt like his heart beating under her touch, so strong and deep and sure.

He took her to the peak and on over it. Once, and again and again after that.

Later, they got up and went back out to the main room, Deck in his boxer briefs and Nell in her black sweatshirt and warm socks. They ate rocky-road ice cream straight from the carton, sharing the spoon, and then ended up on the sofa making love again, eventually falling asleep curled up tight with each other.

She woke well past midnight as he lifted her from the sofa and carried her back to the bed, where he set her on the edge of the mattress and helped her out of her sweatshirt. Then he eased her down to her pillow and pulled off her socks.

"Come to bed," she grumbled. And he did, wrapping himself around her, settling the covers up over them, nice and cozy. "Marriage isn't half bad," she murmured, as sleep crept up on her again.

He cupped her breast in one hand and nuzzled her neck. "Good night, Mrs. McGrath."

Mrs. McGrath. "Not bad at all…"

Rye called her cell at six thirty the next morning. With a sleepy groan, she untangled herself from Deck and grabbed the phone off the nightstand. "This better be good."

"That big Lexus LX of Deck's is down in the parking lot. Thought I should find out if you need rescuing."

The man in question yawned, scratched his cheek and then tried to reach for her.

She laughed and batted his hand away. "Too late. There's no rescuing me now. I've surrendered to the inevitable."

Deck mouthed, *Who is it?*

She whispered, "Rye."

Rye asked, "So what you're telling me is that he's with you and you're good with it?"

"That's right."

"Giving marriage a try, after all?"

Deck tried to tickle her. She swatted the rock-hard bulge of his shoulder and said to Rye, "Yes, we are. He'll be moving in here, so don't freak out if you see him entering my loft."

"As long as he's welcome there."

"He is. I'm giving him a key and the alarm code."

"Must be true love, after all."

"Well, we *are* married."

"All righty, then." She could hear the grin in Rye's voice. "You can go back to…whatever it was you were doing."

"Thanks, Rye." She ended the call.

Deck reached over and snatched the phone from her hand. She screeched in protest and a wrestling match ensued, one that ended with the phone on the floor somewhere and Deck making love to her again, a satisfying outcome for both of them.

A little while later, she brewed them coffee and scrambled some eggs and explained that she would talk to her sisters and her cousin Rory today. "Ideally, we can all five meet for lunch or something. If not, I'll find a way to get with each of them separately and explain everything."

He set down his coffee cup, his expression suddenly guarded. "Explain that we're married, you mean?"

"Yeah." She studied his face across the table. He didn't look happy. "You okay?"

"Fine." He didn't seem fine. He seemed like something was bugging him.

"Tomorrow's Thanksgiving," she said.

"I know what day tomorrow is."

He definitely had something on his mind. She considered prodding him again as to what. But no. When he was ready to share, she had no doubt he would. "Oh, and just so we're on the same page, dinner will be at Clara's. We'll need to be there at two. Is JC Barrels closed tomorrow?"

"Yeah."

"Can you bring whatever things you need back here tonight?"

"Sure."

"We'll spend tomorrow together and go to Clara's from here."

"Works for me." He ate a bite of eggs. "So why not just handle it tomorrow?"

"Handle what?"

"Telling your sisters. Everyone will be there at dinner tomorrow, right? We can tell them all then."

Men were kind of dense sometimes. "Except for my sisters. They need to know today."

He tipped his head to the side, studying her, like a burglar seeking points of entry into a house with a state-of-the-art alarm system. "For some reason, your sisters have to know before everyone else?"

"Yes, they do."

"And your mother? What about her?"

"God, no. We can tell her Thursday. She and Griff are coming to Clara's for dinner, too. It's a first and we're all feeling good about it. Ma's kind of the last family outlier to come back into the fold. Until this year, she's always begged off on the family Thanksgiving. She was feeling guilty, we all think, and rightfully so, after what she did to Sondra."

"Wait a minute. You can wait till tomorrow to tell your mom, but your sisters have to know *now*?"

And this is a big deal to you, why? she thought, but decided not to ask. For the sake of their new marriage, she tried for diplomacy. "It's about closeness. I'm close to my sisters. They're my girls, you know? They support me in whatever I do in life, no question. And they need to know from me, privately, before everyone else, that I'm married. It's bad enough I told Rye, Meg and James first. But today, I will explain everything to my sisters and they will be fine with it."

"Nellie, that makes no sense."

"Not to you, maybe."

"Just wait until tomorrow."

"Yeah, well." She ate a bite of toast, chewing it slowly, then enjoying a nice sip of coffee, after which she set her cup down with care. "That's not gonna happen."

"I want us to do it together."

It all came unpleasantly clear to her then. "So that you can control what gets said, am I right?"

He flashed her a look—annoyed, but maybe just a little abashed, too. Being Deck, he went with annoyed. "You're pissing me off."

"Welcome to married life. It's called compromise, Deck. And we're both going to be doing a lot of it— oh, and as for your fabled need for control? You'll have to let some of that go, I'm afraid. I promise to be patient with you. But, as for my sisters, I'm telling them today."

"I just might have to break into your closet and cut up some of your clothes." Elise narrowed her eyes and tried to sound threatening.

Nell was sitting next to her, so she threw an arm around her and planted a big kiss on her cheek. "Please don't hurt me, Leesie. I'm sorry I didn't tell you first."

Clara, Jody and their cousin Rory all laughed.

By some minor miracle, Nell's sisters and Rory had all been able to make it to lunch at the Sylvan Inn, a cozy restaurant just outside the town limits where the food was good and the atmosphere friendly. It was kind of the go-to lunch place for the five of them—and their sisters-in-law, too, on occasion. They tended to congregate here when important news needed sharing, when big decisions had to be made or life events required that they celebrate together.

Rory said, "Those rings are gorgeous." And everyone sighed in total agreement.

Then Jody said, "I have to ask…"

Nell nodded. "Yeah?"

"Well, you love the guy, right?"

"I do love him." Nell said it out loud and realized she hadn't said those all-important words to Deck, not this time around. She needed to remedy that, preferably soon.

"So then," said Jody, "why keep the option open for an after-Christmas divorce?"

Nell ate a French fry. "If you knew how hard it was for us to even get to this point, trust me, you wouldn't have to ask."

Clara frowned. "Jody's question is valid, though. I mean, now that you're married and you've come to realize that the love is there with him, why not go all in on it? Leaving the door open to divorce takes the focus off making it work."

Nell gave a slow nod. "I get that. I do. But *he's* the one who suggested we try it till Christmas."

Rory said, "He only did it to get you to give the marriage a chance, right?"

"Yeah. And I *want* to give it a chance. But I don't want him running all over me. I mean, the guy is relentless."

"We noticed." Elise got dreamy eyed. "I like that in a man." Everybody laughed. They all knew Leesie was thinking of her husband, Jed, who could give Deck some serious competition when it came to relentlessness.

Jody said, "So what you're telling us is, you're just not willing to give up the divorce option yet."

It was only the truth. "That's right."

Jody prompted, "Because…?"

"He… Well, he hurt me so deep when we were kids. And he did it twice. And I vowed to myself *never again*. I'm not all the way back from that yet. And he did manipulate me in Vegas—no, I wouldn't have married him if I didn't still want him, still *love* him. But he seduced me to the chapel, he truly did. And, as I said, Deck's the one who suggested the Christmas deadline in the first place, though I know he's not happy about it."

"Because he *loves* you." Jody hit her own forehead with the heel of her hand. "And he wants to stay married to you."

"I know. And he's made it painfully clear that he's not looking forward to having everyone know it could be over by New Year's."

"I get why he feels that way," said Clara. "I mean, really. Think about, Nellie. Nobody has to know that you're keeping your options open. It's not their business."

Elise grinned. "Well, except us. *We* have to know. We're your sisters and we have to have all the facts in order to give you the best advice when you need it."

Nell admitted, "Deck *would* be relieved if we didn't have to tell everyone that we made a deal to reevaluate our marriage on the day after Christmas."

Rory said, "Which means that if you just keep that part of it to yourselves, he'll appreciate that you considered his feelings in the matter."

"True. And he would also see that I'm willing to compromise to make things work between us."

"So...?" Jody made the word about five syllables long.

Nell gave it up. "So, all right then, tomorrow we'll tell the family that we got married in Vegas and we're deliriously happy together. And as for the rest of it, they don't need to know."

That night, Nell and Deck went down to McKellan's for burgers. Deck played pool in the back room with Rye for a while. Meg was behind the bar. Nell kept her company between customers.

Later, upstairs, Nell couldn't wait to get her new husband out of his clothes. They kissed their way to the bedroom, shedding clothing as they went. And when they got there, they fell to the bed together in a tangle of seeking hands and eager, endless kisses. They made love fast and hard and hungry—at first.

The second time was even better. They lay on their sides, joined, moving together slow and lazy and endlessly deep. She felt him all through her. He was branded on her heart, the one she'd loved and lost and somehow miraculously found again.

Afterward, he held her close, his breath warm against her cheek, his finger tracing his name among the flowers and dragonflies inked on her skin.

She said, "I saw Garrett this afternoon at the office."

"Let me guess. You told him we got married."

She waved her ring finger at him. Even with the bedside lamp turned down low, all those diamonds caught the light and glittered. "Well, I *was* wearing these…"

"What did you say to him?"

"Just that we got married in Vegas."

"What about full disclosure?"

"I didn't get into any of that."

"And when you told him we're married, Garrett said…?"

"Something along the lines of 'What the hell, Nellie?'"

"That's understandable."

"Yeah, given that I've been insisting for months that I wanted zero to do with you ever again. Not to mention, I've seen him practically daily since we got back from Las Vegas and never said a word about the wedding till today. But then he gave me a hug and said he was glad for us and he knew we'd be happy together. So that worked out."

"Well, all right, then. And how did it go with your sisters?"

"It was great and they were amazing."

He made a low, gruff sound. "Can you maybe be just a little more specific?"

She pulled away to her own pillow, plumping it a little, then snuggled down with a sigh. "They're happy for us—and about the full-disclosure thing? I've been rethinking that."

"You have?" He watched her face closely, as if scanning for clues.

She nodded. "I've been thinking about it and I've realized you're right. I mean, why tell people we're married and then turn right around and announce that it could end after Christmas? They won't know whether to congratulate us or say how sorry they are that it might not work out."

Something happened in his eyes—a softening. Or maybe just relief. "Yeah?"

"Yeah."

He reached out and guided a loose curl behind her ear. "I think I really like being married to you."

She was tempted to indulge in a little lecture on the topic of compromise, maybe get on him again about the two of them going to see his dad—but then, it didn't all have to be one long negotiation. Sometimes you just did what the other person wanted because giving in made you both happy.

And she did feel happy now. Really happy. Just to be lying here in her bed with him, the way married people do.

Instead of launching into a lecture, she asked softly, "So tomorrow at dinner, you want to be the one to make the announcement?"

"I do, yeah." His fingers eased under the veil of her hair. He rubbed the back of her neck, and she sighed in pleasure just to feel his touch. When he gave a tug, she moved in close to him again. He pressed those warm, supple lips to her temple. "Anything specific you want me to say?"

"Nope. It's all yours."

"You trust me, huh?"

Did she? Well, she was definitely working on that, and now was not the time to play it too cautious. Now, she needed to give her all for this life they'd agreed to try to build together.

She tipped her head back enough for a slow, tender kiss. And she whispered, with feeling, "Yes, Deck. I trust you. I do."

Chapter Seven

As soon as they got in the door of Clara Bravo Ames's rambling old Victorian house the next day, Deck knew that his announcement of their sudden marriage would only be a formality. Not only had Nell already told her sisters, her cousin, her brothers James and Garrett, and Ryan and Meg, she was wearing her rings. Females of the species seemed to have radar for sparkly rings—even little girls.

Deck had barely had time to hand Clara the excellent bottle of Zinfandel he'd brought before Darius Bravo's eight-year-old stepdaughter, Sylvie, came flying down the stairs with Quinn Bravo's seven-year-old, Annabelle, right behind her.

"Hi, Aunt Nell!" Sylvie chirped.

"Hey, Sylvie. Annabelle. Love those dresses." Both girls were done up in velvet jumpers with lace-collared, puff-sleeved shirts underneath and bright bows in their hair.

Sylvie grabbed Nell's hand and squealed in delight. "Aunt Nellie, these rings are bee-ootiful!"

Nell gazed down at her fondly. "Thanks. I love them, too."

"Did you get *married*?" Sylvie's big eyes widened even more as she shifted her gaze from Nell to Deck. "Is this your *husband*?"

"Why, yes, honey. He is. This is Declan, but we all call him Deck." Nell wrapped her hand around his arm and grinned up at him, causing the usual tangle of heady sensations—happiness, frustration that he could still lose her, an ever-present undercurrent of desire.

It had always been like this for him, with her. He wanted her so much, the feeling overwhelmed him. For a guy who liked to have things under control, she was kind of a bad choice. And not only because nobody told Nell Bravo what to do.

From that first day in sophomore English class, when she'd turned around in her chair and blown his mind straight out the top of his head with nothing more than a smile, she was everything. He couldn't keep his cool with her. He lost all objectivity.

It hadn't been like that with Kristy. His first wife had seemed so much more his type. She'd been willing to let him make most of the decisions. She was gentle and sweet and understanding. Kristy had been perfect.

She just wasn't Nell. He'd had to face the bleak fact that Nell owned whatever shriveled sliver of a heart he had. So he'd managed the impossible and earned himself another chance with her.

He was not going to blow it this time.

Sylvie chattered away. "My teacher, Miss Delshire, just got married. She's *Mrs*. Ankerly now. And she has pretty rings, too—but not as pretty as yours."

"Let me see, let me see!" demanded Annabelle, who was not only Quinn's daughter, but also Sylvie's BFF.

Deck knew them all, every Bravo in Justice Creek, including kids, dogs, cats, whatever. When he'd mounted his months-long campaign to win Nell back, he'd made it his business to learn everything he could about everyone in her family.

"Aunt Nell! They're so pretty!" Annabelle cried.

Then the two girls put their heads together. Sylvie whispered something and they both giggled, apparently delighted. When they pulled apart, they gazed up at him solemnly.

"Are you our uncle now?" asked Sylvie.

"Yes, he is," said Nell.

"Nice to meetcha, Uncle Deck," the two said, pretty much in unison. One and then the other, the girls offered him their soft little hands. He gave each one a careful shake.

Giggling again, they ran back up the stairs.

"This way." The doorbell was ringing as Nell pulled him into a large bedroom off the entry hall, where coats and wool scarves were piled high on the bed.

"Come here." He guided her around in front of him, took off her pink wool hat and tossed it onto the bed.

She gave a low chuckle as he unwound her pink scarf. Her eyes were as clear and green as perfect emeralds right then, and her cheeks were rosy from the cold outside. And then there was the incomparable sweet scent of her. She took him by the collar of his coat and pulled him closer, whispering, "I can do that myself, you know."

He tossed the scarf on the pile of outerwear somewhere in the general vicinity of the hat. "But I love helping you out of your clothes."

Her lush mouth was right there, too tempting to resist. He captured those soft lips. She sighed and opened for him. As always, she tasted every bit as good as she smelled.

"Well, I have to say, this is very encouraging," said a woman's voice from somewhere close behind him.

Nell stiffened in his arms. Reluctantly, he released her and turned to face Willow and her fiancé, Griffin Masters. They must have just arrived. Both were pink cheeked from the cold outside and wearing heavy coats.

"Happy Thanksgiving, Ma," Nell said with a slightly forced little smile. She nodded at Willow's fiancé as she unbuttoned her coat. "Hey, Griff."

Griffin, a tall, white-haired guy, still handsome and fit at around sixty, said, "Good to see you, Nell." He turned to Deck. "Declan, right? I think we met at McKellan's once."

Deck clasped the other man's hand and opened his mouth to say something cordial and generic. But before he got the words out, Willow gasped.

"Nellie!" she cried as Nell tossed her coat onto the pile. "Is that a *wedding* ring?"

Nell made a low, impatient sound. "Ma. Will you settle down?"

"But…you didn't say a word. I can't believe you're…" Willow sent a wild-eyed glance at Deck. "I mean that you two finally…" Willow was actually sputtering and, from everything Deck had heard about her, she never sputtered. Then she seemed to shake herself. She braced her hands on her hips. "All right. Let me see that ring. Let me see it this instant."

"Ma, come on. You're acting really strange."

"Give me your hand."

Nell gave in and held it out.

Willow grabbed it with a long, dramatic sigh. "Beautiful. Just beautiful." She hauled Nell close and hugged her tight. "Oh, darling. At last. I'm so happy for you, because I know you've found *your* happiness. And that is all I want for my children."

Nell met Deck's eyes over her mother's shoulder. Her gorgeous face showed him everything. Her mom drove her crazy, but the love was there, too. "Thanks, Ma."

Willow took Nell by the shoulders. "When?" She shot a confused glance over Nell's shoulder at Deck. "How?"

"In Las Vegas," said Nell. "Deck swept me off my feet."

"Las Vegas! But that was a week and a half ago."

Nellie got that narrow-eyed, don't-mess-with-me look. "That's right. And your point is?"

"But I had no clue. What is going on?"

"Nothing."

"That's not true. You were already married when you came over to get on my case for telling Deck where to—"

"So?" Nell's lip curled, but not in a smile. Deck read her like an all-caps text. She was about to say something to her mother that she would later regret.

Deck saved her from herself by clasping Willow's arm. "Hey. Don't I get a hug, too?"

Willow blinked—and took the hint. "Oh, yes, you do." He pulled her close. She whispered, "Well done," before he let her go. And when Griffin moved behind her to help her off with her coat, she faced her daughter with her usual serene smile. "However it all came together, I am so happy for you, my darling. I know the two of you are going to have a splendid life because you are and always have been so very right for each other. And I wish you all the joy in the world."

"Thanks, Ma," Nell replied, equally gracious now. "I'm glad you're here, you and Griff. It's nice to have the whole family together for Thanksgiving."

An hour and a half later, they sat down to dinner.

To accommodate so many Bravos, Clara had brought in two extra tables and arranged the seating in a U shape, with an extra table a few feet away for the kids. There was turkey and ham and just about every side dish imaginable. Dalton, Clara's husband, said a short, simple grace after which they all settled in to eat too much and drink really nice wine.

By then, there was no one in the family who didn't already know that Nell had married him in Vegas and he'd moved in with her at her loft. He didn't really need to make a speech about it.

Still, it felt right to say something. After the big meal was over and the coffee and pumpkin pie had been served, he tapped his spoon on his water glass, picked up the last of his wine and pushed back his chair. A hush settled over the table—except for Jody's baby, Marybeth, who slapped her little hands on her high-chair tray and let out a string of cheerful nonsense syllables.

Deck winked at the baby. "Exactly, Marybeth. I couldn't have said it better myself." A ripple of laughter flowed around the table. Deck said, "By now, I doubt there's a single person in this room who doesn't already know that a miracle happened in Las Vegas Sunday before last." He glanced down at Nell beside him. Her eyes shone clear green and those lush lips curved up in a hint of a grin. "Nell said yes. And I rushed her right to the altar before she could change her mind." He raised his glass. "To all of you at this table, thank you for putting up with me the last few months. I know it wasn't easy." There was more laughter. "And I'm sure many of you have wondered when I would finally give up the chase. But the thing is, I couldn't. Because there is only one woman for me. I know I blew it so bad before—twice. But this time, I promise you, I'm going to get this right. Nellie, here's to you." Her smile went full-out and she blushed the most perfect shade of pink. "Thank you for making me the happiest man alive." He drank the last of his wine and sat down again as the Bravos around him laughed and applauded.

Nellie leaned close and gave him a sweet, swift kiss. He was right where he wanted to be, at her side.

Now, if they could only make it last past Christmas.

That weekend, he took her to visit the new house her company was building for him. The exterior walls were up and finished, the roof on, windows and doors installed.

Outside a light snow was falling as they walked through the framed-out, wall-less rooms wearing their heavy coats, hats, boots and warm gloves. He described some of the planned finishes and the rustic chandelier he'd already chosen for the two-story entry.

"Anything you want to add or change," he coaxed, "just say it and consider it done." He was kind of hoping she might make a few suggestions. That would mean she could see herself living here.

She said only that she thought what he had planned sounded perfect.

In the wide-open space that would soon be the kitchen, she asked, "So, last I heard from Garrett, we're on schedule for completion in March, right?" Her breath plumed in the icy air.

He perched on a paint-spattered sawhorse and pulled her up nice and close. "Yeah. Move-in ready second week of March, barring any number of possible holdups."

"Shh. Never say that out loud. Talk about tempting fate." She swayed toward him and he hooked his gloved hands at the small of her back. Even through her down coat, he felt her soft breasts and the perfect inward curve of her waist. She tipped that pretty chin up to him. "I like it here. It has a very open feel."

He kissed the tip of her nose. "Are you saying you think we should just forget about putting in actual walls?"

She laughed. The sound reached down inside him and warmed him up better than a nice, cozy fire. And then she said sincerely, "I think it's going to be beautiful."

Will you be moving in here with me? he thought, but didn't let himself ask. Again he reminded himself that there would be plenty of time to work it all out once they got through Christmas and made it past the deadline.

The deadline.

It bugged him more with every hour that went by. Why had he even offered it? He wanted to renegotiate—more than renegotiate. He wanted to make it go away.

But every time he got close to asking her to forget the damn deadline, he would remind himself that he'd be better off to chill a little, put his focus on making the next month a good one, giving her a holiday season to remember and several weeks' worth of marriage she couldn't bear to walk away from.

If he could manage that, December twenty-six would take care of itself.

That night he took her out to dinner at a nice little place called Mirabelle's. From there, they went on to his 4000-square-foot rented house on two acres of wooded land a couple of miles from town.

She set her overnight bag on his king-size platform bed in the master suite and whistled in approval. "This place is gorgeous. If I didn't know how fabulous your new house is going to be, I would wonder why you didn't just buy this one."

"I'm extravagant," he confessed, and dragged her down across the bed with him.

She stroked her fingertips lightly into the hair at his temple and traced the shape of his ear. It felt so good—her touch, her scent, her body just barely brushing along his. "You worked hard for it." She gave him a light, sweet peck of a kiss. "Might as well enjoy it."

He went ahead and busted himself. "I probably would have bought this one. But the goal was to get close to you. Hiring you to build my house seemed like a surefire way to get a little face time, at least."

"And then I just handed you off to Garrett."

"Really pissed me off."

"But you went ahead with the new house, anyway."

"Yeah, well. By then I'd hired an architect and he'd come up with the design. It was everything I'd asked for—and more. I fell in love with it and I wanted it."

She dipped her head even closer and brushed a kiss against the side of his throat, her lips so soft, just right. Like everything about her. "Because you demand the best, right?"

"You bet I do."

"*We're* the best—Garrett and me. So you got your house and we got your business. Everybody wins."

He captured her mouth—and right then his phone, which he'd dropped on the nightstand next to the bed, started playing a series of beeping sounds.

She pulled back. "R2-D2?"

"It's my sister. She always loved *Star Wars*, so…"

"Cute." She gave him that grin, the one that made him want to help her out of her clothes.

He sat up and grabbed the phone. "Marty. Hey."

"Hey, Deck…" She sounded strange. Apprehensive, maybe?

"What's happened?" he demanded. Nell, still stretched out across the bed, frowned up at him, looking worried now.

At Marty's end of the line, the baby cried. "Hold on a minute." Her voice retreated and he heard her soothing little Henry. "It's okay, sweetie. It's okay…" He realized about then that he hadn't told his sister that he'd married Nell. As he considered how to break the news, Marty came back on the phone. "Deck, I got a call from the hospital in Fort Collins."

He knew then. *Keith McGrath strikes again.* "Dad."

"He fell down some concrete stairs at that apartment complex he manages." A litany of bad words bounced through his brain. Marty went on, "They took him to Fort Collins Memorial."

"Is he dead?" Okay, that was a little too cold and abrupt. Nell's eyes widened in alarm. He brushed a hand down her arm to soothe her.

"No, Deck," his sister said in a chiding tone. "He's not dead."

Nell's frown had only deepened. He stretched out on his side facing her again and mouthed, *He's okay*, though he really didn't know yet what condition Keith was in.

Marty said, "He's got a bump on the head and some bruising. They're keeping him overnight for observation, but he's conscious. He gave them my number as next of kin." The baby fussed some more. He heard her making soft, cooing noises to settle him down.

Deck got the picture. Either he went or Marty would. He sat up for the second time and swung his legs over the edge of the bed. Nell sat up, too. She scooted in close to him.

She would want to go with him.

No way. He wanted her nowhere near his father. Keith McGrath had supposedly changed his ways the last couple of years, but Deck wasn't about to give him another chance to mess things up with Nellie.

Marty said, "Hank's going to drive me up there."

Not happening. "You're three hours away with a baby to take care of. I'm closer. I'll go."

"But I—"

"Don't argue. I'll leave right away." He felt Nell shift beside him but didn't look at her. "I'll call you from the hospital as soon as I've got the whole story."

He heard Hank's voice on Marty's end, though he couldn't make out the words.

Marty said, "Okay."

Deck wasn't sure which of them she was talking to. "Couple of hours, tops," he promised, "and I'll have more information for you. I'm sure he's going to be fine." Because one way or another, Keith always made it through to mess up again.

"Be gentle with him, Deck. I mean it. He fell and hurt himself. He's doing his best now, staying out of trouble. And he's getting old."

"I will be gentle," he parroted, gritting his teeth a little.

"And call me as soon as you know what's going on."

"Got it. Will do." He ended the call.

Nell's hand settled over his. He realized he still hadn't told Marty they were married. But that was the least of his problems right now.

Five minutes ago, life had seemed just about perfect. Now he had an hour-plus drive ahead of him, and his dad to deal with at the end of it.

He twined his fingers with Nell's, turned to meet her waiting eyes and told her straight out, "My dad's been hurt. I'm not sure of the details, but he fell down some stairs. He's at the hospital in Fort Collins and I have to drive up there and take care of whatever needs doing."

She watched his face closely, worry darkening her eyes to bottle green. "But is he okay?"

"I think so. He's a little banged up, Marty said, and he hit his head. But he's going to be all right."

The tension between her brows eased a little. "That's good."

"Yeah." The word had kind of a bitter taste in his mouth.

"Well, then." She squeezed his hand and started to stand. "Let's get going." He didn't move. After a second, she sank back down beside him. "What's going on? Talk to me."

He caught her face between his hands. "Listen…"

Her gaze searched his. And she knew. "Uh-uh. You're not leaving me here. I'm going with you, Deck." Her voice was satin over steel.

"No. That's no good. Just let me handle this and we can—"

"Stop." She ducked from his touch and stood. "This is what I was talking about. This is where you don't let me in."

He rose, too. "Look. I have to get going. We can hash it all out when I get back."

"The whole point of being married is that we support each other, that we're *there* for each other."

"That's fine. I get it. I do. But, right now, I have to go."

"It's not fine in the least." She let out a hard huff of breath. "You're shutting me out, blowing me off."

"How many ways can I say it, Nell?" His voice was colder than he'd meant it to be. But why wouldn't she take a damn hint? "We will talk this over later."

A low growl of frustration escaped her. She glared at him for a hot count of five. Then she wrapped her arms around herself, whirled and stalked to the floor-to-ceiling windows that dominated the room. During the day, they offered a gorgeous view of the mountains. Now, though, they showed only a dark reflection of the bedroom and the ghostly shadow of the moon outside. For a moment, she simply stood there, staring at the shadows in the window. Then she spun back to face him. "I'm not happy with this."

Would she be long gone when he got back?

Bet on it.

Would he really blame her if she left? No. But he couldn't stand the thought of her near his father. And he knew where to find her if she walked out.

He would make it all up to her. Somehow. After he finished dealing with Keith. "I promise you," he said as gently as he could. "I'll make this as quick as I can."

"How quick you make it isn't the issue."

"Nellie. Come on. I can't deal with this now. I have to go."

She turned to the dark window again, leaving him staring at her rigid back. He didn't know what to say to make it better. The only way to do that would be to give in and take her with him.

Not going to happen.

He stuck his phone in his pocket and headed for the door.

Chapter Eight

Nell bit her lip to keep from calling after him.

She stared blindly out the dark window, keeping her arms wrapped tightly around herself as a way to hold herself in place, to keep from racing down the stairs after him, yelling at him to stop being an idiot and let her the hell in, let her support him when he needed her, let her *be* there for him as a wife should.

Marriage.

She had no idea how to do it. But she'd lived through a lot of yelling and carrying on between her mother and father when she was little—no, Ma and her dad weren't married at the time, but they'd shared a house whenever he wasn't with Sondra. And they had a family together. And the way they went at each other, well, even a little girl could tell that was no way to say *I love you*.

So, terrific.

Deck was leaving without her. She didn't have to like it, but she pretty much had to accept it. He didn't want her with him because he didn't want her near his troublemaking father. And that made no sense at all to her. Hadn't he noticed that they were all grown-ups now? She, at least, was fully capable of not letting one poor old man mess with her head.

Deck, though? Apparently not so much.

She stood very still, listening, and heard a door close downstairs. A few minutes later, faintly, she heard him drive away. About then, she realized she'd ridden out here with him and didn't have her truck.

Very bad words did an angry dance through her brain. Because, yeah, she was mad enough at him right then to want to be long gone when he got back.

It was after ten at night. No way would she call up someone in the family to come to her rescue. Maybe an Uber.

She got out her phone—and then just didn't have the heart to call for that car. Instead, she plunked the phone on the nightstand next to a framed picture of her and Deck at the Gardenia Chapel. They were standing in front of that curtain of shimmery crystal beads, she in her white mermaid gown and he in his rented tux. They looked deliriously happy. Sex and champagne will do that to people.

When she'd first spotted it there on the nightstand, she'd been touched that he'd thought to have it framed, that he'd put it by his bed.

Now, she felt sorely tempted to grab it and slap it facedown and not even care if she ended up cracking the glass.

But no. Her husband might be an idiot when it came

to his father, but that didn't give her a free pass to bust up his stuff.

She returned to the window again.

Outside, it had started to snow. She watched the snowflakes blow against the glass and her fury calmed a little, enough that she couldn't help hoping that Deck would drive carefully and that his dad really would be all right.

It was snowing steadily when Deck parked in the lot at Fort Collins Memorial.

Flipping up the collar of his heavy winter jacket, he jogged to the entrance. The wide glass doors slid open automatically. The woman at the front desk said he should have a seat in the waiting area, that the doctor who had treated Keith would come to speak with him soon.

He took a chair and called Marty to let her know he'd made it to the hospital and would call her back as soon as he'd consulted with the doctors and had a chance to see Keith. When he hung up with Marty, he thought about calling Nell. But a phone call wouldn't fix anything, and they could be interrupted at any moment.

However, he *had* left her stranded at his house. Yeah, he wanted to keep her there, to have her waiting for him when he got back so he could make it all up to her.

Somehow.

But trapping her at his house was just plain wrong, and he supposed he'd been a big enough douche to her tonight already.

Plus, the lack of a vehicle wouldn't keep Nell anywhere she didn't want to be. One way or another, if she wanted to leave, she would go.

So he settled on a quick text in which he provided the alarm code for the house, explained where to find the extra house key and the key to the Land Rover in the garage.

She texted back, Thank you. My best to your dad. Drive safe.

Civil. Innocuous, even. Still, her current frustration with him came through loud and clear.

He started a reply. I'm sorry. I just…

It was as far as he got. Explaining himself by text wasn't going to cut it. Better to leave it alone for now.

He put the phone away and wished he were anywhere but there. The minutes ticked by as he watched the lady at the desk hang tinsel and shiny little ornaments on a two-foot fake tree she'd set up on one end of the long counter. She hummed happily along to piped-in holiday tunes. Not even December yet and already Pentatonix sang "White Christmas" everywhere he went.

"White Christmas," my ass, he thought, completely Scrooge-like and unrepentant about it. It had better not get too damn white out there or he'd have trouble driving home.

"Declan McGrath?" A woman in blue scrubs beckoned him. He got up and went to her. "I'm Dr. Farris. Your father is resting comfortably. He's going to be fine. He has a concussion, some bruising and various minor contusions."

"What happened?"

"He tripped over a mop bucket he was taking down a flight of stairs."

Oh, I'll just bet. "Right."

A tiny frown crinkled the space between the doctor's dark eyebrows. Okay, he'd sounded pretty damn cynical. Probably because he was. Keith McGrath had fallen down stairs before. Somehow, that always happened when people he owed money to got tired of waiting for him to pay up.

Dr. Farris asked, "Are you implying there's something more sinister going on here? Do you somehow suspect that your father has been attacked? I did examine him. And I'm telling you honestly that his injuries *are* consistent with a fall."

Deck got the message. She was the doctor. She would be the one to know if Keith's injuries had been caused by something other than a fall. And he really should stop assuming the worst—at least until he'd checked on Keith and found out if he'd been up to his old tricks. Deck shook his head. "No. Sorry. I'm sure you're right."

The doctor regarded him sharply for several seconds and then went on, "Your father is coherent and resting comfortably. Barring any unforeseen complications, we're expecting to release him tomorrow."

"I would like to see him now."

"Of course. This way." She led him through a set of heavy doors and down two intersecting hallways to a room across from a nurses' station. The door was shut. When she pushed it open, the room beyond was dark. Dr. Farris turned back to Deck and whispered, "He's sleeping."

"It's all right. I'll just go in and wait."

The doctor left and Deck entered the shadowed room. He took off his coat, draped it over the bedside chair and sat down. As his eyes adjusted, he watched the sleeping man on the bed and listened to the soft sounds made by the various machines.

Keith, who'd grown thin and wiry as he aged, lay on his back, his face with its crooked beak of a nose turned away, a bandage in his gray hair. He'd banged up an elbow and had a scrape on one arm.

Eventually, he turned his head and opened his eyes. "Declan." He gave a dry little chuckle. "What a surprise."

"You had them call Marty," Deck accused.

"She's nicer to me than you. Marty still loves her old dad."

"She's got a newborn, Dad. Have a little damn consideration."

Keith made a snorting sound—and then flinched. "Hurts like a son of a bitch. They won't give me anything but Tylenol because it's my head." He shut his eyes. A sigh escaped him. "I know what you're thinking. You're wrong. I wrestled a damn mop bucket on concrete stairs. The bucket won."

Deck found himself buying that story now. People Keith ripped off tended to do more damage to his face. "Okay."

His dad opened his eyes again. He stared at Deck, his thin mouth set. Defiant.

"Dad. Go back to sleep."

"You just gonna sit there and watch me?"

"Go to sleep."

Keith let out another tired sigh, but said nothing more. A few minutes later, his eyes drifted shut.

When Deck was sure he'd gone back to sleep, he went out to the waiting area, called Marty and reported that Keith was doing great and they would be checking him out of the hospital in the morning. She said she would be there. He insisted that there was no point in her driving all the way to Fort Collins. He would take care of Keith, make sure the old man had everything he needed.

Marty came, anyway.

The next morning, right after the day-shift doctor had told Keith he could go home, she arrived with Hank and the baby. She handed the baby to her husband and bent over the bed to give the old man a kiss. "How you doin', Dad?"

"Everything hurts," Keith grumbled. "Even my hair." Fondly, Marty patted his shoulder. He asked, "How's my girl?"

"I'm fine, Dad. Never better."

"Let me see my handsome grandson." Hank brought the baby close again and Keith said what a good-looking kid he was.

Deck stood by the window and watched the old man interact with Marty and her family. Really, Keith seemed like your average, everyday granddad, a little goofy for the grandbaby and straight up fond of his daughter. Deck knew he probably ought to give the old man a break now and then. Keith had been behaving himself for a couple of years now, keeping his nose clean since that last stint at Buena Vista for check kiting.

Still, Deck just didn't trust him. He doubted that

he ever would. Maybe, though, he could at least make an effort to be nicer to the guy.

As for bringing Nellie to see him...

His gut knotted up just thinking about it. Uh-uh. He didn't want her anywhere near him. Yeah, okay, he might as well be honest with himself, at least. He might as well admit that he wasn't rational about this. What harm, really, could his dad do to Nellie? No way would she be taken in by Keith a second time.

It was just that Keith had played his smarmy, low-down tricks on her, convinced her what a good guy he was and that all he needed was a few thousand bucks to turn everything around. It generally worked on people when Keith pulled that crap, mostly because Keith believed it himself. And it had worked on Nellie. Keith had shamed Deck to the core, messing with Nellie like that. That betrayal had cut deeper than all the other ways the old man had screwed up as a father.

Deck had never been able to forgive Keith for taking Nellie's money. He doubted he ever would.

Marty, tired circles under her big brown eyes and her butterscotch hair pinned up in a messy bun, came toward him. "Hey, sourpuss, give your little sister a hug."

He pulled her close. She smelled of milk and baby lotion. "You didn't need to come," he whispered in her ear.

"Too late. Already here—now come on, let's get Dad back home."

Marty and Hank drove Keith back to his apartment at the complex he managed.

Deck stayed behind to make sure the hospital bill

came to him. Outside, the snow had stopped. It hadn't piled up much. The roads would be clear. He couldn't wait to get home, find Nellie wherever she'd run off to and make it up with her.

But it wouldn't be right to leave Marty to handle everything on her own.

So he went to Keith's place to help get him settled in. Keith comanaged the building, working with a couple, Dale and Ginny Hill, who had the apartment next to his. The Hills promised they would look in on him and that they could manage fine around the building while he recovered.

Ginny patted Keith's shoulder downright fondly. "You'll be back in your workshop in no time."

Keith nodded. "That's my plan, Gin." He had a shed on the property where he made children's furniture, toys and planter boxes that he sold at local farmers markets and craft fairs.

Marty walked Deck out to his car when he left. As she stood there shivering in the cold, he realized he'd yet to tell her about him and Nellie.

"Hop in," he said. "I'll turn on the heater."

She climbed in on the passenger side. He got the heat going and tried to figure out how to break the big news. "A couple of things…"

"Don't start, okay?" Frowning, she fiddled with her hair, pulling a bobby pin out of her bun and sticking it back in again. "I really do think he just fell down the stairs."

"It's not about that."

Marty gave him the side-eye. "So…you believe it really was just an accident?"

"Yeah."

And his sister smiled full out. "Hallelujah. He *believes*."

"It's hardly a miracle."

"Maybe not to you."

He gave her a look of infinite patience and said, "We both know if he's having trouble managing on his own, he's most likely to call you. And you'll be calling him constantly, checking on him."

She made a wrap-it-up motion with her hand. "So, and…?"

"He seems to be doing pretty well at the moment. But if you think he needs a nurse or something, let me know, okay? I'll find him one."

"Aw." Her eyes got suspiciously dewy.

"What are you making cooing sounds about now?"

"Well, it's just, I know you're not past all your issues with him, but you're good to him, anyway. It's one of the many things I love about you."

He reached across and pulled her close for a quick half hug. When he let her go, she grabbed for the door handle. "Oh, and, Marty, one other thing…" She waited, her eyes expectant. "I got married two weeks ago."

Marty's mouth dropped open. And then she reached across the console and punched him in the shoulder.

"Hey! Knock it off."

She put her hands to her head as though in fear her brain might explode. "What is the *matter* with you? You run your own company, you're a big, fat success. To do that, you *have* to have a pretty good idea of how to deal with people. But when it comes to the ones who love you, you have your head right up your butt. Two weeks you've been married and not a single word to your own sister?"

He winced. "Sorry. You're right. I should have called."

"Oh, you bet you should have. Who is she? Do I know her?"

"It's Nell."

Her eyes got as wide as bar coasters. "Bravo?" At his nod, she burst out, "Seriously? Nell? After all these years? I can't believe she'd ever have anything to do with you again. I mean, I was three years behind you in school, but everybody knows how you wrecked her when you dumped her flat."

"I was an idiot."

"Yes, you were. You *loved* that girl."

"Yeah. And after it didn't work out with Kristy, I finally had to face the fact that I'd never gotten over Nell."

"And she actually gave you another chance?"

"Well, I was pretty persistent." Understatement of the decade, not that he really wanted to get into how long and how hard he'd had to keep after Nell to get her to give him a break. Marty would probably have a good laugh about that.

His little sister used to be so shy and quiet. But since she'd met Hank and things started working out for her, she'd grown more confident, more willing to speak up about whatever she had on her mind. Most of the time, Deck thought that was great.

Right this minute, though? Not exactly.

Marty stared out the windshield, eyes far away. "Nell Bravo. Wow. Just wow. I mean, never in a million years..." Her voice wandered off, which was fine with him. He didn't need a long detour down memory lane. Marty's bun bounced as she turned his way again. "Tell me all about it."

"Uh. We got married in Vegas. It was sudden. We're still kind of, you know, working stuff out."

"What stuff?"

Stuff like whether or not we'll be together by New Years. "God, you are nosy."

She bopped him on the shoulder again. "Bring her to see us—or we'll come to you."

"Well, I was kind of working my way around to that. Nell wants to get together with you, too. Maybe next weekend? You've got the baby, so we'll come down there. I'll check with her and give you a call."

"Okay, now I'm starting to feel kind of happy. You and Nell." Marty's smile bloomed wide. "Don't you just love it how sometimes in life, things work out exactly as they should, after all?"

Marty stood waving and grinning as he drove away.

Deck pulled the Lexus out of the apartment complex lot, went around the block and parked on the next street over. He needed to call Nell and he was nervous about it. Even on a hands-free call, he wouldn't be paying the road enough attention, so he pulled over before he took out his phone.

Did he expect her to answer?

Not really.

Shocked the hell out of him when she picked up on the first ring. "About time you called."

His heart performed some impossible feat in the cage of his chest. Just the sound of her voice did a number on him. Was he a hopeless fool in love? Yeah, and likely to remain so no matter what happened on December twenty-six. "Hey, Sparky."

She made a low, grumbling sound. "I probably shouldn't even be speaking to you."

But she *was*. And that eased the knot in his gut a little, loosened the band of tension around his chest. Suddenly he could breathe again. "Where are you?"

"Oh, no," she scoffed. "I picked up the phone, which we both know is more than you deserve after the way you left. I think that entitles me to get my questions answered first. We can start with the one you just asked me. Where are you?"

He could see her as though she were right there in the car with him—green eyes flashing, that mouth of hers just begging for a scorching-hot kiss. Longing sizzled through him. "I'm still in Fort Collins, but I'm about to head home."

"Your dad? How is he?"

"He's a little banged up, but it looks like he'll be okay. They released him from the hospital and he's back at his apartment now."

"Well. I'm so glad he's all right." She must have realized her tone had softened, because she added more sharply, "But I'm *not* happy in the least about the way you walked out on me."

"I'm sorry."

She let several seconds crawl by before she spoke. "When are we going *together* to see your dad?"

Never. "Can we talk about that later?"

Another silence. And then she conceded with a tired little sigh. "I suppose."

At least she was letting it go for the time being. He relaxed in his seat a little. "Marty and Hank drove up, too. They brought the baby. I told her we got married. She's happy for us. She wants us all to get together. I was thinking we could drive down to Colorado Springs for a visit. A day trip, next weekend maybe— you don't have to decide now. Think it over."

"It should be doable." Her voice was soft again.

He couldn't stop himself from asking, "So then, have you forgiven me?"

"Don't push it, Declan. Come home. We'll talk some more."

He grinned. It felt damn good. "Home meaning...?"

"I'm at your house."

The gray day seemed blindingly bright all of a sudden, full of promise and hope. "Stay right there. I'm on my way."

She greeted him at the door in a long purple sweater, black leggings and soft boots, her red hair sleek on her shoulders. He didn't think he'd ever seen anything as beautiful as Nellie making herself right at home in his house.

She frowned up at him. "You look exhausted."

"It was a long night. I slept in a chair in his hospital room."

Her expression softened. "You're a good son."

"I only went because Marty would have gone if I didn't—and then she drove up anyway, even though I told her she didn't need to."

"A good son *and* a good brother."

He stepped forward and she stepped back. So much for a hello hug, damn it. He shut the door behind him and put on his sad face. "Don't I get a welcome-home kiss for being so good to my dad and my sister?"

She tipped her head to the side and her hair tumbled down her left shoulder, fire red, shining so bright. He couldn't wait to get his hands in it. "Hmm. There's still the little problem of how you took off without me."

"Please?" He tried to look contrite—not for refusing to take her to see his dad. He would say no to that again in a heartbeat. But for having to run off and leave her alone. He did feel regret for that.

"You have no shame." She tried to look severe, but didn't quite pull it off.

He reached for her.

She let him catch her and couldn't hide her smile when he lowered his mouth to hers. He took his time with that kiss, reveling in the simple reality of having his arms around her again. She tasted like apples and coffee, like everything good.

He let her go with reluctance and took off his coat and gloves. "Smells great in here."

"I made minestrone soup," she said. "Hungry?"

The thought of her puttering around his kitchen worked for him in a very big way.

She'd stayed.

He'd been in the wrong and he knew it. And she had to suspect he wasn't going to change. Not on the subject of the old man, anyway.

And still…she'd stayed.

"Sparky." He pulled her close again and kissed her some more. She twined her arms around his neck. He lifted her off the floor and she wrapped her legs around him, too. He turned for the stairs leading up to his bedroom.

But she broke the kiss and put her hand against the side of his face. "When was the last time you ate?"

"I had some eggs at the hospital this morning."

"You need to eat." She smoothed the collar of his shirt in a proprietary way that pleased him to no end.

But there were more important things in the world than soup. "What I need is to take you upstairs, peel off all your clothes and show you what a good husband I can be."

"First, you should eat." She squirmed a little. "Put me down." He gave up and let her go. She grabbed his hand. "Come on. Soup."

She led him into the kitchen, where she pushed him into a chair and filled a couple of bowls with that terrific-smelling soup. There was crusty bread and sweet butter, too. She took the chair across from him and they ate in silence for a few minutes.

"I wanted to go with you last night for *you*, Deck," she said finally.

He ate more bread. It was a much better use of his mouth than answering her, because he wasn't going to say what she wanted to hear.

She took a thoughtful sip from her water glass. "It goes both ways, you know. You don't only take care of me. I take care of you, too. I can't do that if you won't let me—and I know. You were too proud to let me take care of you when we were kids. I can see now how you felt you *couldn't* take care of me and you hated that. But what's the point of finding each other again if we just reverse roles? It has to be both of us, each for the other. That's the only way it can really work."

Her skin was the most gorgeous shade of milky white that turned the prettiest pale pink when she blushed or got turned on. He didn't think he would ever tire of just looking at her. He watched her hand as she set down her water. Slim and white, that hand. But he knew it had rough spots—on her palms and at the joints of her fingers—from building things. He really liked the rub of that slight roughness against his skin.

And what were they arguing about? Right. Taking care of each other. "Sparky, you're here now. You stayed. You made soup. That's taking care of me."

She ate a bite of bread and took a spoonful of soup before she said, "Please just think about taking me to see him. We don't have to stay long or anything." She gazed across at him, so hopeful, so sweet.

And as far as his dad went, they were at exactly the same place they'd ended up the first time they'd had this discussion, the day before Thanksgiving, when she'd finally agreed to give their marriage a real try.

"All right. I'll do that," he lied—and waited for her to call him on it.

She simply shook her head in in a weary sort of way and concentrated on finishing her soup.

He knew a strange, frantic sort of feeling, that she was only playing him along. Yeah, she was being gentle with these ongoing requests to meet up with Keith.

But she wasn't giving it up.

No, she hadn't laid down any real ultimatums on the subject. Still, he definitely felt the pressure from her. The fact that she wouldn't just give it up and leave it alone had him trying to gauge how important a visit with Keith was to her.

Important enough to be a deal killer on the day after Christmas?

No. She'd never draw that kind of a line about it. Would she?

Uh-uh. He was reading way too much into it.

Maybe if she kept after him about it in the weeks to come, he would start to worry.

But one way or another, he'd steer her away from Keith—and still end up married to her when Christmas was over.

As of now, well, why get all tied up in knots about it? Better just not to think about it, to put it completely out of his mind.

Chapter Nine

After he finished his soup, she dragged him into the living room, where she had boxes full of Christmas decorations all ready and waiting, along with a big fake tree for him to assemble.

She explained, "I put the soup in the slow cooker this morning and then I went looking for your Christmas decorations. I checked the closets, the attic and out in the garage. Didn't find any."

"That's probably because I don't have any," he muttered. *Because I don't need any.*

She elbowed him in the ribs. "Don't you dare get grinchy on me."

"Wouldn't dream of it—so you bought all this junk today?"

"Junk?" she mimicked pointedly.

"Ahem. Let me try that again."

"Please do."

"So today you bought all these *gorgeous* decorations and this tree that I'm certain will look terrific over there in the front window?"

"Yes, I did," she announced with pride. "I took your Land Rover out and I went shopping. One of the guys at the Christmas Store loaded the tree box into the car for me. But getting it in here by myself took some planning. After you called and said you were on your way home, I took the tree out of the box and dragged it in here in sections."

"You could've just waited for me."

"I know." She gave him her sweetest smile. "But I wanted to get going on it. I thought we could put this tree up today and do the one at the loft tomorrow night."

"We need trees at both places?" Wasn't one way more than enough?

Not to Nell, it wasn't. "No, we don't *need* them. We *want* them."

"Ah. Good to know."

She slanted him a pouty glance. "Or maybe you're too tired to decorate? Would you rather go upstairs, get some sleep?"

He hooked his arm around her neck and pulled her close enough breathe in the almond scent of her shampoo and press his mouth to the smooth skin of her forehead. "If we go to bed, it won't be for sleep."

"I didn't say *we*, Mr. Scrooge. Whatever you decide to do, I'll be down here decorating."

So that pretty much settled that. If he couldn't give her a visit to his dad, the least he could do was help her with the damn tree.

It took several hours. But, really, it was almost worth all the work. That night, they had a fire in the fireplace and the tree all lit up in the front window. His big rented house had never felt so much like a home.

The next night they were back at her place with another tree to decorate. She had one of those retro aluminum trees for the loft. He stuck the branches in the fat tube that served as a trunk and mounted it on the stand. All the decorations were aqua blue. Nellie had a color wheel that she put on the floor at the base of the tree and it turned slowly, bathing the shiny branches in alternating bands of different-colored light.

"Pretty, huh?" she asked, when they stood back to admire their evening's work.

"Spectacular," he replied drily. "And how come you didn't warn me that when a man gets married he's automatically signing up for a whole bunch of holiday decorating?"

"Are you complaining?"

"Me? No way."

"Good. Because Thursday, we're going to out to Rory and Walker's ranch for their annual family decorating party."

Thursday night at Rory and Walker's, all the Bravos and their husbands and wives were there.

Everyone pitched in to wind garland over every banister and railing in sight. They piled greenery on the mantel and put up those little Christmas villages and miniature snowy scenes on just about every available flat surface. All while an endless succession of Christmas records on actual vinyl played from Walker's old-school stereo system.

Deck decided that it wasn't half-bad. There was hot chocolate. And beer and drinks for anyone who wanted liquor.

And a whole bunch of wedding presents for him and Nellie. Apparently, the Bravos *had* to throw a party whenever one of them got married. With two more family weddings coming up in the next few weeks, opportunities were limited to celebrate an unexpected Vegas marriage.

So Rory had declared that the decorating party would be in honor of Deck and Nell. Elise had brought a wedding cake, three tiers done up to look like a stack of Christmas presents, complete with fancy frosting bows and shiny sugar ornaments. Deck and Nellie cut the cake and smeared frosting on each other's faces. They shared sugary kisses as Rory, who was a professional photographer, took shot after shot.

Much later, at the loft, they opened their wedding gifts, which were mostly household goods, fancy tablecloths and serving pieces, vases and candlesticks, all that stuff married people used now and then, for special occasions. Deck pictured Nell dressing up the table for a dinner party in some distant, happy, hazy future, imagined himself sitting down to eat with friends and family around them, glancing down the full table at Nellie, his wife.

It was so far beyond what he'd known growing up. They'd never had a damn tablecloth on their rickety kitchen table, let alone silver candlesticks and a big, smiling family.

But he would have all that now. And with the woman he'd wanted since the moment he set eyes on her. He should be happy. Proud of himself to have come this far, gotten this close to having everything he'd ever imagined in his wildest dreams.

And he *was* happy. Just with a few raggedy spots around the edges. Because it wasn't a done deal until they got out to the other side of Christmas together.

Nell set down a giant glass vase from Jody and nudged him with her shoulder. "You're wearing your grim face."

What was it about women? They took one look at a guy's face and saw way more than any man ever wanted them to know.

He wrapped his arm around her and nuzzled her ear. "I was just thinking, *Wow, that is one big-ass vase.*"

She let out a little snort of laughter—and then asked softly, "Not gonna talk about it, huh?"

I hate that damn agreement and I wish we'd never made it. How hard was that to say?

Really hard.

He could hit the jackpot. She might answer, *I hate it, too. Let's pretend you never suggested it. Let's call this a done deal and stay married forever and ever.*

Or he could end up making things worse. She might say she wasn't ready to put the agreement aside and then proceed to tell him why—including how she wasn't giving up on that visit with Keith and if he kept refusing to take her to see his dad, she would refuse to stay married to him.

Bottom line? He didn't know what she would say.

Uh-uh. Better just to let it play out, stop being such a weenie about it. One way or another, he would find a way to keep her with him when the holidays were through.

* * *

Saturday, they did Rocky Mountain Christmas, Justice Creek's annual holiday shopping fair on Central Street. Deck enjoyed it. Nellie bought presents for just about everyone in her family and Hank and Marty, too. As for Henry, he got the most stuff of all. Nell bought toddler toys and blue pajamas, onesies and booties and a mobile for Henry's crib. That night, she wrapped everything to take to Marty's house the next day.

It was snowing Sunday morning, but it had tapered off by noon when they left for Colorado Springs.

At Marty's, Nellie put the gifts she'd bought under Marty's tree. They had dinner. After the meal, Hank turned on the game in the living room. Nellie asked to hold Henry. She sat on the sofa with him and he went to sleep in her arms.

Marty pulled Deck into the kitchen, supposedly to help with loading the dishwasher, but really to report that Keith was doing fine and already back at work playing fix-it man around his apartment complex.

"Great," said Deck, ready for talk of Keith to be over and done. "Glad he's feeling better."

Marty was watching him way too closely. "You haven't even told him that you and Nell got married, have you?"

"Why does this feel like the beginning a lecture?"

Marty braced a hand on the counter by the sink and scowled at him. "He's your father, Deck." At least she kept her voice low so Nellie wouldn't hear. "He'll be happy for you."

"Can you just stay out of it?"

"Look. I get it. I know you've still got issues on your issues when it comes to him. And I was there. I remember what he did, hitting Nell up for a 'loan' that you had to pay back. I understand why you don't trust him. But I feel like a liar every time I talk to him. It's big news that his son got married. It's something he should know."

Did he get that? Yeah, maybe. A little.

He blew out a hard breath. "I'll call him tomorrow and tell him. I should check on him, anyway."

Marty smiled then. "Thank you." She tipped her head toward the living room. "You did good, big brother. Nell's a total keeper."

"Yeah. She's all that and then some." *And now if I can just manage not to screw it up.*

Deck called his dad from his office at JC Barrels the next morning and got voice mail. "Hey, Dad. Marty says you're doing fine, already working again, so that's good. Listen, can you give me a call when you get a minute?" He hung up and felt antsy for an hour and a half.

Until Keith called him back.

"What's up?" the old man asked.

Deck rose from his desk and shut the door. "It's like this. I got married to Nell Bravo. It was a few weeks ago—before you fell down the stairs. Marty got after me to tell you. So, well, now you know."

The silence at the other end of the line went on for a while. Finally, Keith said, "Congratulations. I'm happy for you."

"Thanks." The word tasted like sawdust in his mouth.

"She's a good girl, that Nell."

Stay the hell away from her. "She's not a girl any-more."

"You pay her back that money I took off her?"

"I did."

"I figured you would."

"Yeah, well. That's all. I'll talk to you—"

But Keith wasn't finished. "How you and your sister turned out so good, I got no clue. I'm grateful every damn day for the both of you, and that is a plain fact."

"Dad, you don't have to—"

"All I'm sayin' is, it's a comfort, that's all, to know that in spite of what a mess I made, you two will be okay."

What the hell was he supposed to say to that? It wasn't that he couldn't forgive Keith. It was just that he still didn't trust him and didn't know if he ever could. "Well, I just wanted you to know I got married. Give me a call if you need anything."

"Declan?"

"What?"

"You gonna bring that sweet girl around to see your old dad, let me apologize for taking her money back in the day?"

Not a chance. "Doubtful."

Keith took a moment to let that sink in. "Well. You be happy together, you and Nell. She was always the one for you."

Okay, he just couldn't let that remark stand. "If you knew that, why'd you mess with her?"

"What can I tell you? I had the devil on my tail back in those days. I made one bad choice after an-other, until it got so that bad choices seemed like the only kind there were."

"Well, you can't really blame me, can you, if I have trouble trusting you?"

"No, Declan. I can't blame you. I *don't* blame you. Not one bit."

Nell spent that morning at a reno she was supervising for her brother Quinn up in Haltersham Heights. Quinn's passion was his gym, Prime Sports and Fitness, but he flipped houses for profit and he used Bravo Construction to do the work.

When it got close to lunchtime, Nell called Meg. "Where are you?"

"At the loft going crazy."

Nell laughed. "That's a pretty normal state for a bride five days before her wedding. How 'bout lunch?"

"Yes! Please! Now!"

"Twenty minutes, the Sylvan Inn?"

"You're on."

They got a deuce in the corner and the biggest gossip in Justice Creek, Monique Hightower, as their waitress. Monique sashayed over, her blond curls bouncing. "Happy Holidays! Nell Bravo, where have you been? A demolition site?"

Nell wore work clothes and boots, but so did more than one man in the place. "Count your blessings, Monique. At least I washed off the construction dust. How are you?"

"Terrific. I hear congratulations are in order."

"Thanks."

"I mean, really. You and Declan? After all these years. I seem to recall you once said you wouldn't spit on him if he was on fire in the street."

Nell smiled sweet and slow. "Believe it or not, Monique. Sometimes true love does win out."

Monique handed them menus, rattled off the specials—and then turned on Meg, "So the wedding is Saturday, or so I heard?"

"That's right."

"You and Ryan and your whirlwind romance. I hope you'll be very happy."

"Yes, we are. Thank you so much."

The less of Monique the better, as far as Nell was concerned. "You know what? I'm ready to order now."

Meg agreed that she was, too. They ordered sandwiches and coffee and handed the menus back. Monique bustled away.

Meg leaned across the table and whispered, "I have no idea how she keeps her job."

"Sometimes I wonder, too. But then again, what would the inn be without Monique here to drive us all crazy?"

"You're right. And at least she didn't ask what *Clara* thinks about me and Rye." Clara and Rye were lifelong BFFs. They'd even almost gotten married once—at Christmastime three years before. Many people in town believed that Ryan McKellan would always be in love with Clara, who had married Dalton Ames the summer after that almost-wedding to Rye.

Monique appeared with their coffees.

As soon as she was gone, Nell reached across the table and fondly patted Meg's arm. "You get that crap a lot, people giving you innuendo about Rye and Clara?"

Meg only shrugged and dribbled cream into her cup. "Now and then."

"It *is* just crap, you know. Rye loves Clara. But he's *in love* with you."

Meg sipped her coffee and answered easily, "I know."

Nell felt the tears rise—the good kind. She sniffled and waved her hand in front of her face. "I love it— that you love him, that he loves you. That you two just went for it and it's working out so right."

"Yeah," Meg agreed quietly. "He's the man for me. I love Rye, I'm *in* love with Rye. And I trust him."

"Trust…" Nell felt an ache, a bittersweet yearning in the center of her chest as she thought of Deck, of the marriage they were trying to build. Did they have trust, really, between them? He didn't trust her around his dad. And she didn't quite trust him enough to give up the option for an after-Christmas divorce.

Meg fake coughed into her hand and muttered, "Warning. Monique. Closing in behind you."

And then the waitress was there. "Here we go." She slid their full plates in front of them. "Now, what else can I get you?"

"We're set," said Meg. With a giant smile, Monique whirled and bounced away. Once she was busy at another table, Meg asked, "Now what were you about to say?"

Nell picked up a triangle of her BLT. "I was just thinking about Deck and me, that's all. How we seem to be doing everything backward. I mean, we get married on the fly and then we negotiate whether or not to try to make it work."

"But do you trust him?"

"To be true to me? Absolutely."

Gently Meg coaxed, "So what you're really saying is that there are other ways trust is lacking between you?"

"Exactly. I had a few issues growing up. He had it a thousand times worse than I did. We fell so hard for each other in high school. And then everything went wrong. Now, trust is sort of a work in progress with us."

"But you *are* in love with him and he's in love with you. You're it for each other."

Nell poked a stray piece of bacon back into her sandwich. "That wasn't a question, was it?"

"Nope. I know a couple in love when I see one." She picked up a section of her grilled ham and cheese. They ate in companionable silence for a few minutes.

Then Nell asked, "So how was the trip to Oregon?" Ryan and Meg had flown back to Valentine Bay, Meg's hometown in the Pacific Northwest, on Thanksgiving weekend.

"It went well. My parents love Rye. And he got along great with Aislinn and Keely." Aislinn Bravo and Keely Ostergard were Meg's two lifelong BFFs.

Nell said, "I can't wait to meet my cousin." Nell's dad and Aislinn's father had been brothers, though they'd lost touch over the years.

"Won't be long now. Aislinn and Keely are driving in Thursday." The two would share maid-of-honor duties at the wedding. "They threw us a combination wedding shower and bachelor/bachelorette party at the Lighthouse Café, my favorite restaurant back home."

"You miss Oregon?"

"Now and then." Meg sounded just a little bit wistful. "But I love Justice Creek. I'm happy here—and my parents are coming in tonight." She glanced away. "They're staying with us at the loft."

Nell leaned a little closer across their small table. "And…?"

"I love my mom."

"But…?"

Meg groaned. "But she thinks she knows everything and she won't stop with the well-meaning advice. I wanted to get them a room at the Haltersham." The century-old luxury hotel was by far the best in town. "But my mom looked so hurt when I suggested it. So she and Dad are staying with us."

Nell had an easy fix for that one. "Have them stay at my place."

Meg started right in protesting. "No, Nellie. I didn't mean—"

"Don't argue. It's perfect. They'll be right there with you—just not right on *top* of you."

Meg set down her half-eaten section of sandwich. "I was just whining a little, not hinting. We'll be fine."

"I know you weren't hinting. But I *am* offering—scratch that. I'm *insisting*. We'll just stay at Deck's. Better for you, no problem for me. Deck and I are going back and forth between our two places anyway until we figure out where to settle in the end." And didn't that sound reasonable, even if it wasn't the whole story? Now Nell was the one glancing away. She frowned down at her French fries and wondered if that showed lack of trust, too, somehow—that they couldn't even agree on one place to live? Or was she just suddenly oversensitive on the subject of trust?

Marriage. Sometimes it seemed like a lot more trouble than it could possibly be worth.

"Something wrong with your French fries?" asked Meg.

"Not a thing." Nell picked one up and popped it in her mouth. "Your parents. My place. It's the perfect solution to your problem."

After lunch Nell drove home to her loft to pack what she'd need for several nights at Deck's. She tossed her bags in the back seat of her crew cab and went on into the office at Bravo Construction, where she called the cleaning service she used occasionally. They would send someone over right away to change the sheets and spiff things up at the loft for Meg's mom and dad.

Then she called Deck. "Got a minute?"

"For you, a lifetime."

Well, that made her feel all melty inside. "I might just need to keep you around, McGrath."

"Works for me because I'm going nowhere." His rough, low voice caused a slow burn in her lady parts.

"You are a very dangerous man."

"No, just determined."

And relentless. "Um. Where was I...?"

"About to suggest a little afternoon phone sex? Or wait. Where are you? I'll come there."

"Oh, I'll just bet you would." She had that ache again. And not only for sex with him. For *everything* with him. "But I, um, I called to say I offered the loft to Meg's parents. They'll be here this evening, stay through the wedding Saturday and fly back out to Oregon Sunday. Any problem with us moving over to your house tonight for the rest of the week?"

"As if you even need to ask."

"I didn't think you'd mind too much," she muttered wryly. He was such a caveman. And he wanted her in *his* cave.

"You know..." All of a sudden, his voice had turned way too casual. "We could simplify everything if you just moved to my place permanently."

Why did saying yes to that tempt and terrify her simultaneously? "Not ready to do that yet."

"Yet." His voice was rough again. She wanted to rub herself against it. "Meaning you will be, eventually."

I think so, yes. She should say it out loud.

But her trust?

As of right now, it wasn't quite there, and she wasn't letting him push her too fast. "We need to get groceries."

If it bothered him that she'd changed the subject, he didn't let on. "I'll pick you up at the loft. We can stop at the store on the way back to the house."

"Deck. I need my truck—you know, to go to work, get around. Because this is the twenty-first century, and women have lives and jobs of their own."

"You can have the Land Rover."

"Thank you, but I want my *own* car."

"You sound about twelve. About twelve and sticking out your tongue at me. Makes me want to give you a spanking."

"I believe I am mildly offended."

"Only mildly? Good. I can work with that. This could be hot."

"Hold that thought. Until tonight."

"Spoilsport."

She laughed. It felt so good, teasing him. Making

simple plans with him—to stay at his house, to stop on the way home for groceries.

And as for having him as her partner in life...

Warmth flooded through her. She wanted that. Wanted *him*.

So why was she hesitating? Why not just throw out the damn agreement and go all the way, promise him forever and get to work on the rest of their lives?

"Sparky? Still with me?"

She put all the tough questions away and answered, "Right here. Get whatever you need from the loft and meet me at Safeway. Five thirty. Customer-service desk."

"I'll be there."

And he was.

They grabbed a cart and rolled up and down the aisles like your average married couple out getting the groceries on a weekday evening.

She bought a holiday centerpiece of roses, pine-cones, holly and amaryllis as the store PA system played Christmas tunes. To "The Little Drummer Boy" and "Santa Baby," they argued about what to have for dinner. And they forgot the eggs. She had to run back for them after they'd already unloaded everything onto the checkout belt.

She followed him home and—yep, she'd started calling his place home in her head. So that was another little step toward forever, wasn't it?

It had started snowing again. By the time they reached the house, it was coming down pretty steadily.

Deck pulled his car into the garage, got out and ran back to her in the driveway. She rolled her window down.

He said, "I'll move the Land Rover and you can pull in."

"Thank you." She tipped her head out the window, offering a kiss for his thoughtfulness. He met her halfway and she reveled in the cold bite of snowflakes on his soft, warm lips.

Inside, he turned up the heat and she turned on the tree. They put the groceries away. He made *pasta e fagioli*. They sat down at the breakfast-nook table with the soup, a bottle of wine and a loaf of French bread.

It was all so homey and comfortable and natural. She was happy, in his warm house with the snow falling outside, her festive centerpiece on the table.

And with Deck.

Deck, whom she'd lost so long ago. The man she'd put behind her for good.

And yet here she sat at his table. She slept in his bed.

Deck. Her husband.

Of all the impossible, terrifying, wonderful things.

"Have I got soup on my nose?" He had on that crooked smile she loved so much—a little bit rueful, a whole lot sexy. "You're staring at me."

I love you, Deck. I always did. I never stopped.

It felt good to think it. It felt *real*. She should let it out, say the words, share her growing acceptance of him in her life, share her joy in the happiness they'd found together since those wild nights in Las Vegas.

She opened her mouth to say it, *I love you.*

But then she had a sudden flashing vision of her younger self, drenched to the skin in a hard summer rainstorm, trudging through the mud, arms around her middle, huddled into herself, letting herself cry now that he couldn't see her doing it. Because he was behind her in his ancient pickup, following her even though she'd told him to go, even though all she wanted was to get away from him. All she wanted was never to set eyes on him.

Not ever again.

That long-ago summer day had broken her. That day had shown her that there was no hope for her with him. She had to be done with him.

She couldn't love him anymore. They were finished. Forever. She'd given him everything, all she had, keeping nothing back. He'd thrown her away, anyway.

A girl had to learn a lesson from that. From heartbreak like that, a girl learned to be more careful, to keep a closer watch on her vulnerable heart.

Now, she met his eyes directly across the table and answered his question. "Your nose is clean." *But I am not ready yet to give you everything I have again.*

Life was so painful and strange. At eighteen, she'd been eager to take on forever with him. But he'd walked away. And now he finally wanted everything with her.

She couldn't do it, couldn't give herself completely. She just didn't trust him. Not all the way—and really, he didn't completely trust her, either. If he did, they would be going together to visit his dad.

"Don't," Deck said in a low growl. "Don't go away. Don't shut me out." He knew her so well, knew she'd retreated into her doubts, left him sitting there at the table, across from her but alone.

"I'm right here," she lied. It wasn't constructive, behaving this way. Far from it.

And he wasn't having it. "Uh-uh," he said. "No

freaking way." He slid his napkin in by his bowl, shoved back his chair and rose to loom over the table. "If you're going to run off inside your head, the least you can do is tell me why."

She pushed her bowl away.

"Say it," he commanded.

She lifted her hands—and then let them drop limply. "Look. I want to trust you."

"But you don't." The words dropped into the space between them, heavy as stones.

She confessed, "No. I don't fully trust you not to hurt me again, just like you don't trust me not to mess up with your dad somehow."

"What will convince you that I know I screwed everything up and all I want now is a lifetime to prove to you that it will never happen again?"

"Time, I think. I just need time."

"Nellie." He spoke so patiently, standing there across the table from her, not the least bit cocky for once. "That's what we're doing. Giving it time—and as far as my dad goes, it's *him* I don't trust, not you."

Anger shivered through her. "Oh, please. What's he gonna do? He can only manipulate me if I let him. And I'm not going to let him."

His burning gaze dropped then. He stared down at his almost-empty bowl as though wondering how it had gotten there. "I'm just…" The sentence wandered off.

Impatiently, she finished for him. "Not ready?" When he didn't look up, she added, "Well, neither am I. And however it all shakes out, it's good, you know? You and me, this Christmastime together. I'm glad for it. I really am."

He did lift his head then. His gaze caught hers, held it fast. "You and me, Nellie. That's all I want."

I want that, too.

But she didn't say it. She couldn't give him what they both wanted yet. She just wasn't ready to take that next step.

"You and me, Nellie," he repeated, his voice rougher, more demanding. "You need to get used to it. You need to admit it. You're mine and I'm yours. Even the way I messed up when we were kids hasn't changed that. Eleven years apart, and here we are, right where we were always meant to be."

She didn't argue. It sounded so good. She wished…

But all she could give him was, "I hope you're right."

With a low oath, he came for her.

She waited for him, her gaze never wavering, every nerve tingling, her skin supersensitized, sudden, sweet heat blooming low in her belly.

Okay, maybe he *had* seduced her to the altar, and maybe they each had issues they hadn't resolved yet. Who could say what would happen on the day after Christmas?

But right this minute, they shared what she'd given up all hope of ever having with him. Right this minute, they had each other, in a warm, safe place, a tree in the front window, the snow drifting down outside.

When he reached her, she rose to meet him. And when he pulled her close she tipped her head up, eager for his kiss.

Deck's kiss.

Nothing like it.

A perfect, ever-deepening kiss.

A kiss that swept her away to a lush, carnal world where doubts melted like snowflakes on warm skin.

He framed her face in those big hands and he claimed her with his soft lips and his seeking tongue. It was so good, the feel of his hands on her, the taste of him, the heat of his breath, the forceful way he took her mouth. She swayed against him.

He grabbed her up and lifted her right off the floor.

Hooking her ankles at the base of his spine, she plastered her body hard and tight against him. He wrapped her up in those giant arms of his and kissed her all the way to the living room. At the fireplace, he eased her down onto her feet again and went to work getting her out of her clothes.

He had her naked in a minute and he tossed his own clothes on top of hers in a tangled pile. And then he kicked it all out of the way and took her down to the soft rug in front of the fire.

"Come closer," she whispered.

"I'm right here." He licked the outer shell of her ear, tracing the curve of it all the way down to her earlobe, which he bit—gently at first.

And then harder.

She moaned and nuzzled closer still, licking a trail up the thick, beard-bristled column of his throat, over his square jaw and then catching the corner of his mouth in a hungry little kiss. He turned into that kiss, fully claiming her lips all over again.

They rolled and she was on top.

She took advantage of the dominant position, sliding off him to kneel at his side, pressing kisses down the center of his deep, strong chest. Following the tempting trail of hair along his rocklike belly, she moved on down to where he was waiting, hard and proud, for her to curl her eager fingers around him, lick the salty tip of him.

And slowly take him deep in her throat.

Rising onto his knees, he held her head in his hands, wrapped her hair around his fingers, said dark, dirty, sexy things as she drove him toward the peak—and over.

She swallowed every drop.

And then, with a final rough groan of satisfaction, he pulled her back down with him and cuddled her close to his side. The fire kept them warm until he'd recovered enough to start all over again, tipping her chin up with a finger, settling his hot mouth on hers.

She moaned at the sheer wonder of it. His scent of dark spice was all around her, and she gave herself up to the joy that he brought.

"Nellie…" He kissed her name onto her lips.

And then he rolled her under him. He wouldn't let her up until she'd lost herself completely to the touch of his knowing hands and the wet, hot demand of his skilled, seeking kiss.

She was limp and pliant as a happy rag doll when he picked her up and set her down on top of him. For a little while, she used him as a giant, hot, hard pillow, her legs draped to either side of him, her head cradled on his chest. She listened to his heartbeat.

And she thought that this, right now, was happiness, the two of them naked and satisfied together, in front of a cozy fire.

The future? Who needed it?

This, right now, was everything.

He combed her tangled hair with lazy fingers. A knowing chuckle escaped her as she felt him, tucked against the core of her, rising once more.

"It's so crazy, what you do to me." He pulled her up so he could catch her lower lip between his teeth, so he could whisper a dark command, "Take me, Nellie. Do it now."

No problem. She was wet and so ready. With an easy roll of her hips, she had him where she wanted him.

Whispering impossible sexual promises, he slid those hands down over the twin curves of her bottom, his wonderful fingers gliding in, finding the liquid heart of her. Spreading her wider, he surged up into her, filling her completely in one hard, high stroke.

They groaned in unison then, as she pressed down and he pushed up. Finding the rhythm, they rocked together toward a glorious explosion of bliss.

He went over first, his arms banded so tight around her. "I love you, love you forever, Nellie," he vowed as he came.

Her finish took fire from his. The words of love filled her head.

And I love you, Deck. Always. You're the one, the only one. There's never been anyone who means what you do to me. So many years without you. I don't know how I did it. I don't know how I'll bear it if we don't make it work this time…

She wanted to say it, to tell him everything. Her heart cried for her to confess it all.

Why not? Every word was true.

Yet she held the words back.

She just wasn't ready to go that far. Some still-wounded part of her didn't quite trust him enough.

Chapter Ten

The next day they woke to a clear sky and a foot and a half of snow on the ground.

They stood on the front porch in their pajamas and heavy socks, sipping their morning coffee, blinking against the glare of the sun reflected off that wide, sparkly blanket of white.

Deck took a slow sip of coffee. "Looks like a snow day to me."

Shivering a little against the cold, she sidled up closer to the warmth of his body. "It's just so beautiful."

He wrapped an arm around her and brushed a kiss into her hair. "Come on back inside…"

In the house, he turned on the big screen over the fireplace and they learned that the schools and most Justice Creek businesses were calling it a snow day, too.

Before they sat down to eggs and toast, Deck sent a group email to everyone who worked for him, letting them know that Justice Creek Barrels officially had the day off. Nell called Garrett, who agreed that Bravo Construction would be closed, as well. And then she called Meg to make sure her parents had arrived before the storm.

"They got in safe and sound late yesterday as planned," Meg reassured her.

After breakfast, they put on their snow gear and Deck led her out to the big shed in the back. He had a pair of snowmobiles in there, all gassed up and ready to ride.

They spent a half hour buzzing around the property as she familiarized herself with the controls. When she felt comfortable going farther afield, they headed up the twisting road behind the house and eventually into the forest, where the snow wasn't deep enough to ride.

When they had to stop, he suggested they leave the machines and continue on foot for a while.

They started climbing, weaving their way through the tall, dark trees, moving higher up the mountain. Eventually, they emerged onto a lookout point.

Far below, Justice Creek was picture-postcard perfect, like one of those Christmas village scenes at Walker and Rory's holiday decorating party.

Deck, at her back, wrapped his arms around her and rested his chin on her shoulder. He rubbed his rough cheek against her soft one. "It's a beautiful little town."

"I wouldn't live anywhere else." She turned her head back to him and they shared a quick kiss.

The clouds had gathered again. Snowflakes drifted down out of the gray sky.

"Ready to head home?" He pressed his cold lips to the bit of bare skin between her wool hat and her thick scarf.

Reluctantly she nodded. They started back down.

By the time they reached the house, the snow had stopped again. They put the snowmobiles away and shoveled snow for a while. The shoveling devolved into a snowball fight. He was merciless, firing those fat, frozen balls at her as fast as he could grab them up. She did a lot of shrieking and ducking behind trees, leaping out now and then to get him a good one, preferably right in the face.

They even made a snowman. He was a little lopsided, with sticks for arms and a tipped-up row of coffee beans for a smile.

Late in the afternoon, they went back to bed and made love for hours, getting up only for sandwiches and soup. And then heading right back to bed again.

It was a good day, lazy and easy and fun. They didn't talk of the future, of what would happen after Christmas. There was only the two of them, together right now and happy to be so. She wished it would never end.

The next day, real life intruded. The sky and the roads were clear, and they both went to work.

Friday, the day before Rye and Meg's wedding, Nell had lunch with her sisters and Rory at the Sylvan Inn. Meg came, too, and brought her two best friends from Oregon.

Keely Ostergard owned an art gallery in Valentine Bay. Aislinn Bravo, who was slim and delicate, with big, haunted eyes, looked European, somehow. Both boyish and sophisticated, Aislinn resembled some glamorous French actress—Marion Cotillard. Or Audrey Tautou.

Aislinn and Rory had a lot in common. Aislinn loved the tiny principality called Montedoro on the Mediterranean coast where Rory had been born and raised. Aislinn, as it turned out, had been born there, too, when her pregnant mother gave birth earlier than expected during a visit to the villa of a Montedoran count.

While Rory and Aislinn shared stories of Montedoro, Nell leaned close to Meg and asked how it was going with the visit from the parents.

Meg laughed and whispered, "Let me put it this way. The wedding's tomorrow and I can't wait—and not only to be Ryan McKellan's bride."

Saturday in the early evening, Meg married Rye in a tiny log church up in the National Forest. She wore a cream-colored lace dress and a winter crown woven of small white flowers, lacy cedar branches and red berries. She had only Keely and Aislinn as her attendants. Walker stood up as his brother's best man.

In the front row, Meg's mother cried through the ceremony. Mostly, she cried softly, but now and then a sob or a sudden snort would get away from her. When Meg's dad tried to hush her, she moaned, "I can't help it, Todd. Our little girl is all grown-up…"

After the ceremony, the guests followed the bride and groom along a lantern-lit path to the reception in a rustic, barnlike building not far from the chapel. It was all so charming and romantic. Rye and Meg had never looked happier. Nell teared up a little to think that Rye McKellan had found exactly the right woman for him at last.

The next day, Aislinn and Keely set off for the long drive home to Valentine Bay. Meg's parents drove their rental car back to Denver, where they boarded their flight to Portland.

Monday, Meg and Rye were leaving for their Christmas honeymoon in Hawaii. Nell stopped by their loft in time to say goodbye and to help carry suitcases down to the car. As soon as they were gone, she went back up to her own place to see if she needed to call the cleaning people again.

The loft was spotless. Nell changed the sheets and then called Deck at JC Barrels to remind him that they had dinner at her mother's house that night. Griffin's grown children and their families would be there.

"It's at seven," she said.

"No problem. I'll be home by six at the latest. We can go together."

She found herself wondering which place he meant by "home."

"We're at my place tonight, remember, all week? Until Friday?"

A silence and then a hard sigh. "Can we just give that up? What's the point? We're comfortable at my place. And it's getting old, having to drag stuff between two houses."

He was right on both counts. She kind of wanted to give in, stay at his place, eliminate the extra hassle of moving back and forth. And, more and more, she found herself thinking of his house as home, of how much she would love moving to the new house when it was completed.

But some part of her resisted, the part that still doubted, still couldn't quite trust. They'd made an agreement and she really did need what he'd offered— until Christmas—to decide finally if she could make that big leap into forever with him.

"Nellie?"

She realized she'd been quiet for too long. "I'm here. And you're right. I do like it at your place and going back and forth is extra work..."

"But?" The single word had a hard, angry edge.

"Come on, Deck. We had an agreement."

He said something vaguely obscene under his breath and then, more clearly, "Agreements change."

All of a sudden, she felt miserable. Her heart thudded uncomfortably beneath her breastbone and her stomach had tied itself into a knot. Were they about to have a fight on the phone?

She didn't want to fight with him. She *loved* him.

Even if she did still have issues with him, even if she had yet to tell him she loved him out loud. "Yes, agreements do change," she said as gently as she could manage. "But both people have to be willing to make that change."

"And you're just not." It was an accusation.

"Be reasonable. It's not fair for you to get on me for wanting to stick with the plan."

"I hate the damn plan."

Then you should never have suggested it, she thought, her own anger rising. Somehow, she kept herself from actually saying those bitter words.

A moment later, she was glad she'd kept her mouth shut, because he gave in. "All right." He sounded like a weary traveler in the middle of a long trip down an endless, winding road. "I'll be at your place at six. We'll stay there until Friday, the way we agreed."

She'd won the point.

Shouldn't she feel better about that? "We could compromise."

"How?" He sounded wary, but interested. Definitely an improvement over tired and pissed off.

"We could stay at your house for another week and then move to my place through Christmas…"

In his office at JC Barrels, Deck was silent on his end of the line. He understood that she was trying for compromise. Still, he glared at the bookcase made of wine barrels on the opposite wall.

Christmas. The deadline.

It was flying at them way too fast. Only two weeks to go now.

In two weeks, she would decide whether to stay married to him.

Or not.

"Deck?" she asked hopefully.

"I'm still here," he growled into the phone as he got up from his desk chair, crossed to the bookcase and picked up a blue geode bookend that Marty had given him several Christmases ago. It was heavy, that geode, and would make a satisfying crash if he pitched it at his office door.

Nell added hopefully, "If we did it that way, instead of moving back and forth four times, we would only have to do it once."

Carefully, without making a sound, he set the geode back on the shelf. "You're right." Plus, they'd been at his house all last week when they should have been at her place, what with Rye's parents staying at the loft. "It's more than fair."

"So…?" She sounded so sweet. And he loved her too damn much. They were so close to having it all. No way was she leaving him two weeks from tomorrow. He wouldn't allow it.

Except that he *had* made that agreement. He'd given his word. He didn't see how he could rationalize not keeping it.

And who did he think he was kidding, anyway? She was Nell. She did what she wanted and no man alive would make her stay if she was bound to go.

He needed to take her to the old man. If he did that, she would see it as proof of his trust. He could win her promise of forever that way, he knew it.

But he still didn't want her near Keith McGrath. He just didn't. He didn't give a good damn if the need to keep her away from Keith was irrational. Okay, Keith seemed to have cleaned up his act lately. Didn't matter. The old man had run one too many scams in his day. His father didn't deserve to breathe the same air as Nellie—and if Deck had any say in the matter, Keith never would.

"Hey," Nell said softly, calling him back to the here and now, where she was still waiting for his agreement as to where to stay, when.

"All right," he said. "We're at my house till next week and then your place through Christmas."

That night at the Bravo mansion, Nell was impressed with her mother's efforts to make the big family dinner fun for everyone.

The long table in the formal dining room seated

twenty-four. It wasn't big enough. Willow had brought
in two more tables and Estrella, the housekeeper, had
arranged them, as Clara had at Thanksgiving, in a U
shape. Every seat was taken.

Willow had invited the whole Bravo family that
night—her children, her stepchildren, their spouses
and kids. Rory and Walker came, too. Griffin's two
sons and his daughter and their families had flown up
from California the day before to stay until the wedding on Saturday.

Already, Sylvie and Annabelle Bravo had made
fast friends with Griffin's seven-year-old grandson,
Hunter, *and* with his eight-year-old granddaughter,
Nicole. The rest of Griffin and Willow's grandkids
were babies—except for Clara and Dalton's two-and-
a-half-year-old, Kiera.

Little Kiera spent the cocktail hour following the
older kids around. More than once, her voice could be
heard calling out above the laughter and chatter of so
many guests, "Sylvie, Belle! Wait for me!"

Estrella had outdone herself with the Christmas
decorations. A brilliantly lit tree stood in each of the
downstairs rooms, presents spilling out from under
them in bright, beribboned piles. Swags of greenery
looped along every railing. The mantels were decked
out festively, too.

Willow had even hired a singing piano player to
fill the house with holiday tunes. She beamed at the
chaos of everyone talking at once, of children laughing and running all over the place. She never turned
a hair when Hunter wrestled with his cousin Nicole,
upsetting a side table and sending an antique vase
crashing to the floor.

Instead, she just waved a slender hand and called out, "It's okay! Accidents happen. Careful of the glass, now," as the mothers scooped up the apologizing children to whisk them away from the broken glass, and one of the helpers Estrella had hired for the evening rushed in with a broom.

At the dinner table, Ma's surprising new sweetness continued.

"Beautiful, Griff," she enthused, after her fiancé said grace. "Everyone, I can't tell you what it means to me to have all of you here."

Nell leaned close to Deck and whispered, "My God. I think I see an actual tear in her eye."

"Be nice," he chided. "And what's that in *your* eye?"

She swiped the moisture away, leaned close to him again and whispered out of the side of her mouth, "I have the occasional sentimental moment. My mother? Not on your life."

"She's happy with Griffin, with the whole family around her."

Nell glanced along the table at the many smiling faces and thought of all the years of family turmoil. "There was a time I would have called you crazy if you'd tried to tell me that, someday, we'd all end up here together, sharing a really nice holiday dinner before my mother remarried and gave the mansion to Sondra's children."

"She's happy," Deck said again, all soft and coaxing.

Nell surrendered to the sweetness of the moment. "Yeah. Yeah, she is."

* * *

The next day, Nell got home to Deck's house before he did. She picked up the mail from the box out by the main road, including something from Keith McGrath in a plain, business-sized envelope. In the house, she left Keith's letter with the rest of Deck's mail on the end of the kitchen counter and got busy cooking dinner.

An hour later, Deck came in from the garage still in his winter gear just as she was taking the lemon chicken out of the oven. "Smells good in here." He came up beside her and eased her hair away from her neck with a gentle swipe of his gloved hand.

And then his cold lips touched her nape.

She bumped him with a hip. "Back off. This is hot."

"Yes, ma'am." He waited until she'd set the chicken on top of the stove and then he reached for her.

She laughed as his arms went around her. "Your nose is cold."

"Kiss me, anyway."

She happily complied, sliding her hands up to meet around his neck and tipping her mouth up to meet his. When he lifted his head, she surged up again to brush one more kiss across those wonderful lips of his. "Dinner in ten minutes."

"I'll hang up my coat." He turned for the front hall—and stopped at the end of the counter to check out the mail, picking up the envelope from Keith first. "What's this?"

"From your dad."

"I see that."

She busied herself checking the rice and getting down the water glasses to fill before she took them to the breakfast-nook table. He simply stood there, frowning at that white envelope.

"You think maybe it's a bomb?" she teased, trying to sound totally offhand because she was all too aware of the tension in the way he held his shoulders, in the slight frown that creased his brow. She tried again, straight-faced this time. "Deck. Just open it."

He slanted her a look—distracted. Annoyed. "Later." He took his mail, including the unopened letter from Keith, and headed for the front of the house. When he came back, he'd gotten rid of his coat and gloves as well as the mail.

She set the bowl of steaming rice on the table—and then just had to ask, "Well, what was it?"

He gave a cool shrug. "I have no idea. I didn't open it."

She considered what else she might say on the subject, but couldn't come up with anything especially helpful. Talking about Keith rarely went well.

He asked, "Want wine?"

She decided that the wisest move at this point was to just let it go. "Love some. I put a bottle of Pinot Grigio in the fridge…"

It snowed that night. And it snowed again on Wednesday and on Thursday, too.

But by Saturday, the day of Willow and Griffin's wedding and also the night of the annual Holiday Ball, the roads were clear and the world-famous Haltersham Hotel in the shadow of the Rockies, with its white stucco walls and red-tile roof, glowed with light in every window.

Willow and Griff had reserved two of the hotel's

smaller ballrooms—one for their simple marriage ceremony and one for the reception dinner.

At five that evening, Hunter Masters, the ring bearer, led the way down the aisle. Four flower girls—Sylvie, Annabelle, Nicole and Kiera—followed Hunter. Each little girl wore a red velvet dress, white tights and shiny black Mary Janes. Tiaras sparkled in their hair. The girls marched solemnly down the aisle to where Griffin and Hunter waited for the bride. Each girl carried a white basket filled with red rose petals. They scattered the petals as they went.

More than one guest whispered how well-behaved they were—even little Kiera. They were all four so beautiful and sweet and solemn, marching to the altar and taking their places on the far side of Hunter. Now and then, Kiera was seen to fidget. But she had her idols, Sylvie and Annabelle, on either side of her. They alternately soothed and shushed her. She reveled in the attention—and kept pretty quiet, too.

Then came the bride in a stunning, simple sheath of Christmas-green velvet, diamonds at her throat and sparkling in her ears. She carried a bouquet of pinecones, evergreen boughs and red winter berries.

Nell, in the first row of chairs with Deck at her side, started crying about then. It was all just so perfect and so very beautiful—and why in the world hadn't she remembered to bring tissues?

Deck wrapped his arm around her and pressed a white handkerchief into her palm. Gently, he curled her fingers over it and then dropped a kiss against her temple.

Right then, her love for him felt so huge inside her, like it could crack her ribs and burst right out of her chest. She lifted her head enough to kiss his fresh-shaved cheek and whisper, "Thank you."

Then, carefully so as not to end up with mascara smeared down her face, she dabbed at her eyes as her mother said "I do" for the second time—to a tall, handsome white-haired gentleman who seemed to make her happier than she'd ever been before.

After the ceremony, they all moved to a room across the mezzanine, where the tables were set with gold-rimmed china, gold flatware and tall candlesticks twined with Christmas greenery. Elise, the event planner of the family, had coordinated with the hotel to create Willow's wedding and this reception dinner. Nell caught her half sister's eye across the room. They grinned at each other, all the battles they'd once fought in that look, and the unbreakable friendship they shared now, as well.

It's perfect. Nell mouthed the words at her sister.

Elise, beaming, returned a slow nod.

The champagne flowed freely and just about every adult had a toast to propose as the children ran in and out between the tables, giggling and sometimes tussling with each other.

"Oh, let them play," Willow would insist whenever any parent tried to step in and settle them down. "They're just having fun…"

Eventually, dinner was served. The kids sat down—for a few minutes, at least. They drank their milk and shoveled in spoonfuls of mashed potatoes. And quickly got back up to play some more.

Once the dinner dishes had been cleared away, the staff served coffee and rolled in a four-tiered fantasy of a cake frosted in snowy white and decorated with marzipan poinsettias. Rory took pictures as Willow and her groom did the honors. They were like a couple of giddy kids, Ma and Griff, giggling and mugging for the camera as they stuffed each other's faces with cake.

Finally, Willow thanked everyone for making her wedding the happiest day of her life. It was after eight by then and the Holiday Ball was about to begin. Parents took the kids home.

Everyone else headed for the main ballroom, stopping off first in the ballroom's lobby to check out the silent auction, which occurred every year at the Holiday Ball.

This year, the auction proceeds would go to the local animal shelter, the Pet Adoption Project. The shelter had approached every business in town to donate prizes. All kinds of cool pet stuff had been the result, including a bunch of imaginative pet beds, toys and play structures. Bravo Construction had donated a catio, a fully enclosed outdoor space with cozy sheltered areas and climbing runs where pets could play outside, protected from predators and safe from the temptation to wander off. Justice Creek Barrels had donated a whiskey-barrel doghouse and a wine-barrel dog bed.

Nell stroked the curved wooden sides of the doghouse. "It's beautiful. I always wanted a dog…"

"Me, too." He ran a slow finger down the side of her throat, stirring lovely shivers as he went. "Maybe we should get one."

She almost said yes—but then she thought of the deadline. Better to wait until that was settled. "Maybe. In the New Year…"

Something flared in his eyes—frustration? Resentment that she'd yet to throw out the deadline and admit she couldn't live without him? But all he said was, "I'll hold you to it."

"A dog's a big responsibility."

"That's right. A dog is a long-term commitment." He slipped that big hand around her neck and tugged her closer. They shared a quick kiss. "What kind of dog would we get?"

"Well, we would just go to the Pet Adoption Project, find one we both like, a friendly dog, a short-haired one, I think."

"A big one?"

"Midsize."

He kissed her again. "Midsize will do." He tugged on a curl that had come loose from her updo. "I'll tell you what's beautiful, Sparky. You are. I love this dress." It was cobalt blue satin, a simple, full-length strapless sheath.

Her heart kind of stuttered inside her chest and a sweet shiver raced down her spine. She fiddled with the collar of his snowy dress shirt and those all-important three little words rose to her lips. *I love you.* She actually opened her mouth to say them.

But then he took her hand. "Let's dance."

They went through the wide, carved doors into the Haltersham's main ballroom, where the chandeliers were authentic Tiffany art glass and the windows, topped with graceful fanlights, looked out on the crescent of silvery moon suspended as if on a string above the dark mountains.

The band had a keyboardist this year. They were playing a dubstep version of "Deck the Halls." They'd turned the Tiffany lights down low and a strobe flashed on the packed dance floor. Deck pulled her onto the floor and they bopped around to the crazy beat, laughing and having a great time.

After several fast songs in a row, the band finally played a slow one. Deck gathered her close. They swayed to "All I Want for Christmas," and she wished she could capture the moment, like a scene in a snow globe, the two of them dancing. Married. Together. At the one and only Haltersham Holiday Ball.

Monday, Willow called Nell. Griff's family had already left for Southern California. Willow and her new husband were leaving the next day. They would spend Christmas in San Diego.

"Come for lunch here at the house," her mother offered—well, it was more of a summons, really. And that had Nell suspecting that Willow planned to offer some annoying bit of motherly advice.

Didn't matter, though. Not really. Nell wanted to see her mother anyway, to wish her well and say good-bye.

Willow would be in Southern California until after the holidays. She would return only to collect the few things from the mansion that she wanted to keep— and, after that, to visit now and then.

Griff wasn't there when Nell arrived, which made her even more certain that Ma wanted a private talk, just the two of them. Estrella served them chef's salads and hot homemade bread in the dining nook off the kitchen.

Willow chattered away, about how happy she was, about her fondness for Griff's family and for her own stepchildren, too. She laughed at that. "Who knew I would end up loving Sondra's children?"

Nell felt her eyes fill. Lately she seemed to tear up over everything. "Never in a million years," she agreed. "But loving your stepchildren looks good on you, Ma."

Eventually, Willow did get around to the subject of Deck. "He's a good man—and he's always been the *right* man for you. You need a guy who can keep up with you. I'm so glad you two finally got back together."

"Yeah. We're happy. Together. It's working out great." They were. And it was. And so why did she sound so limp and pitiful when she said it? She loved him, deeply. Completely. More so, if that was even possible, than she had all those years ago. And yet something within her still held out against telling him she belonged to him, against promising him all of her days, now and forever.

Ma asked, "What is it? What's holding you back, Nellie?"

Did life get any weirder? She was actually considering confiding in her mother.

And then she did it. She admitted, "I guess I'm still not completely over how bad he hurt me way back when."

Willow sipped her sparkling water. "It's understandable. I mean, at the time, you and the rest of your brothers and sisters were furious with each other and with your lives—and with me and your father, too—for a number of valid reasons. Back then, you never willingly told me what was going on with you. But even I knew that Declan had cut you to the core."

"Everybody knew."

Willow reached across and laid her hand on top of Nell's. "You sat in your room for weeks. You never washed your hair and you lived on Cheetos and Mountain Dew."

"Ma, he hurt me so bad. It was the deepest, dirtiest kind of blow—not only to my heart, but to my sense of myself as a person worth loving. And now, I just can't stop myself from wondering, what if he does it again?"

Willow gave Nell's hand a gentle squeeze before pulling away. "He won't. He's a grown man now. He's ready for a strong woman like you. Plus, look how hard he's fought to get another chance with you. That man is not going to mess it up with you again."

"How can you be sure? How can *I* be sure?"

"I'm so sorry, baby girl. I don't have the answer to that one. I'm fresh out of guarantees. But I do think that at some point, you just have to do it, go for it. You have to let yourself love full out, to open your heart wide and give the man you love your trust. Yes, that will mean you give him the way to hurt you the most. But it's also the only way to real, lasting happiness with another human being."

Chapter Eleven

Nell left the Bravo Mansion at a little after one. Her work schedule that afternoon was light, with no appointments. She called Ruby just to make certain there was nothing she needed to deal with right now.

"Nope," Ruby said. "There's nothing that can't wait till tomorrow."

"All right then, I'm taking the afternoon off."

Nell headed to Denver, where she bought Deck his Christmas present.

She got back in time to meet him at his house at six for the move to her place. They would live at the loft until Christmas, so she boxed up everything under his tree to take with them.

Stuck between a present from Marty wrapped in gold foil and another from Clara and Dalton, she found the envelope from Keith. Apparently, Deck had stuck it there the other day for reasons that made zero sense to Nell. She dropped the envelope into the box with the other gifts.

The box full of gifts was big and unwieldy, so when they got to the loft, she had Deck carry it up the stairs. She opened the door for him and ushered him in ahead of her. "Go ahead and unload it, would you?"

"Sure." He carried it over to the tree and set it down.

As he knelt to do the job, she reminded him, "That letter from your dad is in there."

"I know." He didn't look up, just kept picking up bright packages and shoving them under the sparkly aluminum tree.

"You threw it under the tree at your house?"

"That's right." He still didn't look at her.

It was probably a good time to just let it go. But that unopened letter annoyed her no end. Okay, he had problems with his father, but what if there was something important in there? "You ever plan to open it?"

He did look at her then, a swift glance tight with impatience. "I'll open it at Christmas with the rest of the presents. How 'bout that?"

"It's a present?"

"How the hell would I know? I haven't opened it yet."

She put up both hands. "Well, all right, Mr. Cranky Pants. Guess we'll find out what's in it at Christmas."

"Nellie…" At least he sounded a little bit sorry.

Not that she cared. "There's more stuff in my truck." She turned for the door again.

He was up and across the room in about a second and a half. "Hey…" He caught her arm.

"Let me go. I have things to do." But she made no move to pull away.

He slid his hand up under her hair, gathered her close and pressed his lips to the spot between her eyebrows. The tender little kiss felt good—even if she did find him totally exasperating. In a sexy, manly, irresistible kind of way.

"Sorry," he whispered. "I'm an ass."

"Yeah. Pretty much."

"Forgive me?" He tipped up her chin. "Please?"

She whispered, "Yes," as his lips met hers in a slow, sweet kiss.

It seemed to Deck that he could feel her resistance, that she still wasn't sure yet, wasn't ready to promise him the rest of their lives.

Christmas was a week away and he couldn't figure out how things would go down at the deadline. It was driving him crazy. He wanted to talk to her about it.

But what was there to say?

Are you staying with me, Nellie?

Such a damn, simple question.

Except, what if she said no?

He just needed to stop thinking about it, let it be. Enjoy her and what they had together, face her decision when the time came.

They finished bringing everything in and putting it away. She suggested they go down to McKellan's for dinner.

Later, in bed, it was as good as it had ever been. Better. Every time was better.

In the morning, she scrambled eggs for their breakfast. She made them so light and fluffy, but not too dry.

Exactly the way he liked them.

They went to work, came home. Bought groceries. Shared a meal, went to bed.

It was all so ordinary, their life together. Ordinary in the most perfect way. It was all he'd ever wanted, really, even when he'd thrown it all away. A good life with the right woman—with Nellie.

A dog, maybe, midsize with short hair, as they'd planned at the Holiday Ball. And, someday, a kid or two.

Why did time always go by so fast when you only wanted to make it slow the hell down, when you wanted every minute to last?

All of a sudden, it was five days till Christmas, then three, then two.

On Christmas Eve, Nell's half sister Elise and her husband, Jed, threw a little party at their place for family and friends. It was several couples and a few single friends, pretty much everyone in their circle who didn't have kids yet. They had dinner and then they went downstairs to Jed's man cave, where they played pool, pinball and video games. Elise's enormous cat, Mr. Wiggles, draped himself on top of a tall corner cabinet and looked down on the party through narrowed amber eyes. Elise had put a silly elf suit and hat on the big guy. That cat wore it in style.

Back at the loft, they made love by the fire. And then, a second time, in bed.

By then it was two in the morning.

Christmas Day already. Dread had curled up tight in his belly, a rattler ready to strike.

"Get some sleep," she whispered, and turned off the lamp.

"Come here." He hooked an arm around her waist and pulled her flush against him, her back to his front, spoon style. She snuggled in good and close, her perfect butt right where it would do the most good, perking him up all over again.

He nuzzled her hair. "You smell like Jordan almonds. I love Jordan almonds."

"It's my shampoo."

"It's so damn sexy…"

She took his hand and eased it up between her beautiful breasts. "I mean it," she scolded in a whisper. "Go to sleep."

He cradled one breast, pressed his nose even deeper into her fragrant hair and closed his eyes.

It was going to be all right. It had to be. If she had it in her head to leave him, she wouldn't have made love with him twice tonight, would she?

She wouldn't let him hold her like this, so close, so intimate.

So absolutely right…

"Declan. Oh, Declan…" Nell's voice, in a sweet little singsong, teased him awake.

Was that coffee he smelled?

He opened one eye to a slit—enough to see her standing over him in her flannel snowman pajamas and a giant, floppy cardigan, a steaming mug between her hands.

"Merry Christmas." She smiled down at him.

Deadline day—or more specifically, their last day before the deadline. One way or another, by tomorrow, she would decide.

And right now, she *was* smiling. So far, so good. He asked hopefully, "Is that coffee for me?"

"Yes, it is." She laughed and backed up, holding out the cup. "But you have to get up to get it."

He threw back the covers and swung his bare feet to the rug. "Gimme that."

She backed up another step, taking one hand off the coffee mug and using it to make a show of fanning herself. "Put something on. When you're naked, it's too hot in here."

He would have made a grab for her, but then she might spill the coffee and it looked scalding hot. So he got up and strolled to the bureau against the far wall. He took out a pair of sweats, his ancient waffle Henley and some heavy socks, and put them on as she stood there, watching him, a teasing smile on those lips he never could wait to kiss. She looked downright adorable. Plus, she had coffee.

Once he was dressed, she let him have the mug. He took that all-important first sip. "This might be heaven I'm in right now." He paused to sniff the air. "Is that breakfast I smell?"

She crooked a finger at him and backed toward the door. "This way…" And she led him to the main room, where the table was all set. "Here you go." She pulled out his chair for him.

"I'm liking this." He sat down and she served him. "Eggs Benedict." He couldn't resist putting out a feeler. "Okay, that does it. This needs to be a Christmas-morning tradition." He held his breath waiting for her answer.

"Merry Christmas," she said again, and leaned in

for a kiss, one he thoroughly enjoyed—even if her answer told him zero about how things would shake out.

The food was amazing. He focused on that, on enjoying every bite, on staying firmly in the damn moment, on not thinking of how if she chose to leave him, he would have to let her go because he'd given his sworn word on that, straight up.

And he couldn't go back on his damn word now.

He cleared the table. She turned on the fire and the rotating light for the tinfoil tree. She queued up the Christmas tunes, putting them on nice and low. Beyond the tall windows, the snow was coming down thick and fast.

"Time for presents!" she crowed, clapping her hands like a kid.

"You're really into this," he grumbled, because she enchanted him and maybe he would lose her tomorrow, and if that happened, he had no next move.

"Oh, yes, I am!" She grabbed his hand and towed him over to the sitting area closer to the fire and the big windows with the nice view of the mountains through the swirling snow. "Sit." She pushed him down to the sofa. "Stay." With another happy giggle, she hustled over to the tree and came back with a present. "Here you go. Open it."

It was from Marty. He untied the big purple bow and ripped off the shiny paper. Inside was a Pottery Barn box containing a three-tiered server. "Just what I always wanted," he said without a whole lot of enthusiasm.

"I love it." Nell took it from him and set it on the kitchen counter. "You can put fruit on it." *You?* Did that mean he would be using the damn server alone because she wasn't staying? Or was it just a universal-type you?

"Great idea." He set the empty box aside and went to the tree, returning with a box wrapped in silver. "This one's yours."

"Thank you." She beamed him a sweet smile.

As she opened it, he went and got the rest of the presents he'd chosen for her. There were a lot, because he wanted to give her everything, and when it came to her, he had zero restraint.

There were Louboutin boots and a Fendi bag, a fur-trimmed Prada puffer jacket and a Blancpain Quantième Retrograde watch set with diamonds, the face made of mother-of-pearl. There were also several lacy bits of La Perla lingerie—yeah, okay, the bras, thongs and see-through body suits were more for his pleasure than hers.

But she got all excited over them, anyway. She jumped up and announced that it was way too much and he shouldn't have—but she loved it all anyway, every one of the gifts he had chosen for her. "This watch, most of all. Oh, Deck…" She already had it on and she gazed down at it adoringly. "It's amazingly gorgeous even if it did cost too much. I love that you've got one and my dad had one. And now, so do I." She kissed him.

He kissed her back. And for a moment, he almost forgot that he could lose her tomorrow—come on, how could he lose her? In no way did she seem like she planned to go.

She wouldn't be showering him with kisses and jumping up and down over the watch he'd given her if she planned to call it off tomorrow.

Would she?

But then again…

Maybe he just had no clue what she was really thinking.

It had been that way for her, hadn't it, both times he'd left her?

He would never forget that look of pure shock on her face the first time he told her they were through. To her, it pretty much must have seemed out of nowhere. She'd confessed that she'd loaned Keith five thousand dollars.

And he'd just waited until she stopped apologizing and said, "That's it, Nell. We're finished."

She'd given him that look then—stunned. Mortally wounded. Like he'd taken a knife and shoved it straight through her heart. *But…I love you, Deck. You love me. We're forever.*

Yeah, well. None of that matters. I'm through with you. It's over. We're done. And he'd walked away—just left her standing there with her mouth hanging open.

For weeks after that, she kept showing up wherever he went, trying to get him to talk to her. He always refused.

And then nothing. For a while, she left him alone. He didn't know which was worse—her popping up everywhere or not seeing her at all.

Then came that summer afternoon, the air thick with ozone, dark clouds heavy in the sky.

He'd been working at the pizza parlor over on East Creekside Drive and found her waiting outside for him when he finished his shift that day.

"Please, Deck. I just need to talk to you. Just talk to me, that's all."

He should have said no the way he had every other time, just said no and walked away fast.

But he'd missed her so much, like there was a giant, gaping hole inside him that only she could fill. So he'd taken her for a ride out to their special place.

And when he stopped the pickup, he reached for her. She'd landed against his chest with a happy cry and she'd gazed at him so tenderly, green eyes full of hope and a fierce, bright joy. She had thought they were making up, that this was a new beginning for them.

Because no way would he make love to her only to send her away all over again. What kind of lowlife would do something like that?

She didn't understand that it was only a moment of weakness for him—not until afterward, as she was putting her clothes back together. He'd glanced at her sideways, furtive and guilty, because he felt like such a jerk.

And it had happened again. She got that look of pure shock, as though he'd struck her a killing blow. That time, the look only lasted a split second.

Then she got mad…

Now, all these long years later, on Christmas morning with the snow coming down outside, she'd never looked happier. She was humming along to "Rockin' Around the Christmas Tree" as she opened a gift from Garrett and his wife, Cami.

Deck got up and poured them more coffee.

They'd almost made it through the big pile of packages. There remained one good-sized, brightly wrapped box tied with a giant green bow—and the damn letter from Keith that he should have opened days ago. He picked the letter up off the floor and returned to his chair.

She rose, got the box and carried it back to the sofa, where she sat down again, this time with the box in her lap. "This one's for you," she said, her smile blindingly bright. "It's from me." He started to set the letter aside, but she put up a hand. "No. You go ahead. This can wait another minute."

He tore open the envelope.

Inside, he found one sheet of paper—a short note scrawled out by hand. And a check. His stomach heaved and rolled when he saw the amount.

He set the check on the little table next to his chair and read the note to himself.

Son,
I'm happy for you that you finally got back with Nell. She was always the one for you and I know that I'm more than a little to blame for the way it worked out between you and her years go.

It's been eating at me all this time, that I took money from her. Like a lot of things I've done in my life, it just wasn't right.

I know you said you paid her back, so I am paying you back. I know it isn't anywhere near all you've had to pay in your life for something that was never in any way your fault—for a simple accident of fate, having me as your old man. But this check is good in the way that I know matters to you, because I earned the money honestly, selling stuff I made with my own two hands.

You be happy. That's all I want for you.
Sincerely,
Your dad

Deck couldn't breathe suddenly.

It was too much. All of it.

A check for five thousand dollars from the old man. And this letter.

This letter that brought back too damn many ghosts of Christmas past.

And Nell, too. Nell on the sofa with a Christmas present for him, looking so beautiful, his lifelong dream come true—as tomorrow came flying at him way too damn fast.

"Deck?" she asked from across the coffee table and a thousand miles away. "Deck, what does it say? What's the matter?"

He couldn't do it. Not right this minute. He just couldn't deal. He dropped the note on the coffee table. "I need some air." And he got up and headed for the door.

His boots were there. Moving on autopilot, he pulled them on. He grabbed his heavy jacket off the peg and shrugged into it, took his keys from the little dish on the entry table and dropped them into a pocket of the coat.

"Deck! Wait…"

But he couldn't wait. Not until he had some fresh air and a moment or two to himself.

He opened the door, stepped through, pulled it shut behind him and made for the stairs—not the ones to the parking lot. The other ones that led to the door that opened onto the sidewalk in front.

Down he ran. At street level, he shoved the door wide into a wall of freezing wind and blowing snow.

The door shut and locked automatically behind him. For several seconds, he just stood there sucking in air hard and fast as wind and snow whipped around him, blowing his coat open, the snow sticking in his eyelashes, icy cold on his cheeks.

His head spun with images. The glow on her face just now, when she'd opened her presents, how bad he'd hurt her back in the day, the sad, desperate Christmases when he was a kid, especially the worst one—Marty grabbing his arm, whispering frantically, *No, Deck. Dad said to stay right here...*

It was ridiculous.

He was ridiculous.

He needed to get away for a while, get straight with himself, clear his head. Nell wouldn't stay with him, he was sure of that now. What he'd done to her in the old days, it was too wrong. She couldn't possibly forgive him. He was going to lose her again and he had no idea how to keep that from happening.

Talk about irony. He had it all now, everything he'd worked so hard for. Everything but Nellie to share it with.

Through the whirling snow, he could see his Lexus, waiting where he'd left it at the curb, across the street and down. It was still early on Christmas morning—no other vehicles, no people in sight—so he just walked in the street, moving at a slight diagonal toward his car, his mind locked on Nellie, on her beautiful face, on how he would lose her and how he *deserved* to lose her.

The big vehicle came at him from behind. He heard

tires screaming and glanced over his shoulder just in time to see the terrified face of an unknown woman through the windshield.

It happened so fast.

One second he was trudging along, arms folded across his chest against the wind, images of Nellie flooding his brain. And then, out of nowhere, he was flying through the air.

Chapter Twelve

His ass hit the windshield. He felt the weird give of the safety glass as it broke into a web of tiny pieces without actually shattering. There was a faint scream from somewhere—the woman behind the wheel, maybe.

And then he was bouncing again, up onto the roof of the vehicle. He put his hands down to break his fall and managed somehow not to crack his skull open. And then he was rolling again. Some blind instinct for self-protection surfaced. Ducking his head, drawing his knees up and in, bringing his arms up to protect his skull, he somersaulted back over the roof, whacking his left arm a good one as he went. There was a hot bloom of pain on the outside of that arm, midway between his elbow and his wrist.

But he was still rolling, over the back of the vehicle

and down to the frozen ground behind it. He landed hard—on his ass again. The impact shot up his spine. He let out a groan.

Stillness. The vehicle had stopped and so had he. He sat in the middle of the street, his head down, knees drawn up, left arm cradled against his chest. That arm hurt like a son of a bitch.

Time got weirdly distorted. For some unmeasurable length of it, he just sat there, cradling his injured arm, wind and snow whipping around him.

He heard the slam of a car door. A moment later, someone was standing over him. "Omigod! Oh, my Lord! Are you all right?"

He made himself look up. It was the woman he'd seen through the windshield. "I think my arm might be broken."

"Omigod!" she squealed again. "Oh, I'm so, so sorry. You were just walking. In the street. I didn't expect that. And the snow was so thick. By the time I saw you it was too late to stop and I…" She let her voice trail off as she knelt beside him, cell phone in hand. And then she gasped. "Ambulance. I should get an ambulance." She punched up three numbers and put the phone to her ear.

And then he forgot all about her.

Because Nell was there. "Deck." She knelt on his other side. She had on that puffy coat he'd given her a half an hour ago. Her hand clasped his shoulder and she asked so gently, "Where are you hurt?"

The lady from the SUV was babbling out information to whoever she'd gotten on the other end of the line.

He just stared at Nellie. God, she amazed him. Just

looking at her made his heart hurt in the best kind of way. She had her red hair tucked under a purple wool hat and she wore those snowman pajamas shoved into a pair of winter boots. Her nose and cheeks had already turned red from the cold.

"Deck, can you hear me? Are you hurt anywhere?" Her eyebrows were all scrunched up in worry over his dumb ass.

"I'm pretty sure I broke my arm, but other than that, I think I'm all right."

"Your head...?"

"You won't believe this. I managed to fly through the air and roll over the back of an SUV and *not* hit my head—and we should probably get out of the street before another car comes along."

She unwound the wool scarf she had around her neck. When he scowled up at her in confusion that she'd suddenly decided to start taking off her clothes, she explained, "For a sling," and got right to work knotting it around his neck, creating a cradle for his bad arm.

"Nellie," he said, still stunned at the miracle of her presence when he'd already reconciled himself to the loss of her. "You're here..."

"Of course I'm here. Now, come on. Let me help you..." She took his good arm and eased it across her shoulders. "Ready?"

"Yeah."

He groaned at the effort and staggered at first, but she hauled him upward and helped him hobble to the sidewalk behind his Lexus. The lady from the SUV trailed along behind them, still talking on the phone.

"We should get you to the hospital," said Nell.

But the woman who'd run into him pulled the phone from her ear and said, "Don't move. An ambulance is on the way." As if on cue, they heard the siren in the distance.

The EMTs stabilized Deck's arm and put him in the ambulance. Nell stayed behind to talk to the guy from Justice Creek PD. The officer asked for Deck's identification, so she went back up to the loft and found it on the dresser in the bedroom. While she was there, she grabbed her purse, too.

Back downstairs, she gave the officer the license, answered his questions and got insurance information from the woman who'd run into Deck. Then, finally, she headed for Justice Creek General.

By the time she got to the emergency room, they'd already x-rayed Deck's arm and given him something for the pain. The ER doctor explained that Deck had a nightstick fracture of the ulna—the outer bone in the lower arm. It was a simple break and Deck was lucky. Most likely, no surgery would be required. The doctor performed closed "reduction," meaning he manipulated Deck's arm to realign the two broken pieces of bone, and then he put on a splint.

In a few days, when the swelling went down, Deck would visit an orthopedic specialist who would probably replace the splint with a cast. In the meantime, the doctor prescribed over-the-counter medications and ice packs applied often for thirty minutes at a stretch.

It was early afternoon when they released him. The nurse took Deck out in a wheelchair—hospital procedure, she said. Nell got her truck from the parking lot and picked him up by the front doors.

He didn't say much during the short ride home. When they got there, he seemed to have no trouble getting up the stairs, and that eased her worry for him a little. A broken arm was no fun, but it could have been so much worse.

In the loft, she wanted to put him to bed, but he insisted he was hungry and would eat at the table. He iced his arm as she heated up soup and made them grilled-cheese sandwiches.

"Feel like a nap?" she asked, when he'd finished his food.

He caught her hand as she reached down to take his empty soup bowl, and an arrow of love for him pierced straight through her heart. "Turn the fire back on." He kissed the back of her hand. "Sit with me on the couch."

She had him brace his injured arm on a pillow, draped a fresh ice pack over it and sat with him. He wrapped his good arm around her. She leaned her head on his shoulder and felt such gratitude, that he was here with her, that he was all right.

He asked, "Did you read that note my dad wrote?"

She tipped her head back enough to brush a kiss on his beard-scruffy jaw. "No. I almost did, to see what had freaked you out so bad. But then that seemed wrong. He didn't write it to me."

"I want you to read it."

That was good, right? That he would share it with her? "Okay." She picked up the single sheet of paper from the coffee table where he'd dropped it before he ran out into the snow. It only took a minute to read it. The simple, heartfelt words made her eyes blur with tears.

"I know you have…problems with him," she said. "But this is a *good* thing that he did, Deck—this letter and the money, too." She tipped her head toward the check he'd left over on the side table.

"You're right. It's a good thing." Deck pulled her close again. "It was…bad when Marty and I were kids. And after my mom died, it got even worse."

She pressed her hand against his chest. He felt so warm and solid. Safe. Here. With her. "I knew it. Though you never would talk about it."

"He never beat us or anything. He loved us, he did. He just… Every cent he got had to go into some big scheme. We were hungry a lot. And he was always gambling and borrowing. Sometimes he gambled or borrowed from guys who took it out on him with their fists when he didn't pay up. He would come home with black eyes—and worse. One time, at Christmastime, a couple of guys he owed money to came to the house."

"Oh, Deck. That's just so horrible and wrong…" She reached up and laid her hand against his cheek.

He gazed down at her, but his eyes were faraway, lost in what had happened all those years ago. "We survived. And we're a lot better off now—Marty and me and Dad, too."

"But still…"

He eased his good arm out from around her and clasped her hand instead. They twined their fingers together. "That time they came after him at the house, I was twelve. It was the year after my mom died. We had this little tree. They knocked it over, smashed up the ornaments. I was hiding with Marty in her closet and we could hear the ornaments breaking out in the living room. Marty begged me to stay put, but

I couldn't stand it. I came out screaming for them to leave my dad alone, leave *us* alone. I yelled at them to stop breaking our tree. One of them popped me a good one right in the jaw. I went down, but then I jumped back up. The guy who'd hit me laughed. And then he hit me again. My dad was begging him to stop, to leave me alone."

"That's so awful. I just can't even imagine it—and wait. What about Marty?"

"She was always smarter than me. She stayed in the closet until they were gone." He let go of her hand to smooth his palm down her hair. "And, yeah, that guy who hit me knew what he was doing. But they gave up and left before he did any permanent damage. I had a few bumps and bruises, but I was okay."

"You were just a kid. It must have been terrifying." Reaching up, she wrapped her hand around his neck and pulled him close, nose to nose. "But all that's over now. You're an amazing man and I love you. I love you so much, Deck."

He went very still then. His eyes burned into hers. "You mean it, Nellie? You're not gonna leave me tomorrow, after all?"

She tried to sniff back the tears, but they wouldn't be held in. A couple escaped and trailed down her cheeks. Tenderly, he brushed them away. She sniffed again. "Deck?"

He kissed her wet cheek. "Yeah?"

"I want you to open your present now, please."

He studied her face as though committing it to memory. "All right. I would like that."

She picked it up from the end of the sofa where

she'd dropped it when she ran out after him. "Here you go. You need help? I mean, your arm and all…"

"I think I can manage."

It took him a little while one-handed, but he got the bow off and tore the pretty paper away to reveal a white box. He removed the lid. Inside, on a fat bed of wadded-up tissue paper was another, much smaller box. She'd wrapped it in pretty paper, too. And tied it with a satin bow.

He slanted her a glance.

She said, "That's the *real* present."

He smiled then, and she saw that dimple in the corner of his mouth, the one that told her everything was good with him. "You're such a tricky girl." He untied the bow on that one and tore off the paper with his teeth. "Damn," he said, when he saw what was inside. "Nellie."

She took the velvet box from him and flipped back the lid to reveal a thick platinum band. "I mean, since we're staying married, you really need a ring. I want all the other women to know they'd better keep their hands off my man."

He breathed her name so softly then—"Nellie," like it was the only word he knew.

She leaned across him and slipped it on his left hand. "There. It looks really good, I think. Even with the splint."

"Nellie."

She lifted up enough to kiss him. He wrapped his good arm around her nice and tight. "Merry Christmas, Deck."

"I love you, Nellie."

"And I love you."

Hope and happiness shone in his eyes. "You and me, that's what you're saying, right? You and me forever?"

She nodded, kissed him again and then rested her head on his broad chest. "That's right."

His warm breath stirred her hair. "And a midsize dog, maybe kids later?"

"All of it, Deck. We're going to have all of it. I'm in it, all the way, with you. I want this marriage, want to make it work, to make a life at your side. The 'till Christmas' deal was a bad idea. I was a coward, afraid to just say yes, let's go for it. Let's make it real. I was afraid you would hurt me again, afraid to put my heart on the line. I'm not afraid anymore—scratch that. I'm terrified. But I do love you. You're the man for me and I want to share my life with you and only you."

"That's what I want, too. All of it, with you. And Nellie, I know I let you down, since we got back together. I should have trusted you more, should have taken you to see the old man like you asked me to."

She shook her head. "I pushed too hard on that, same as I tried to push you to marry me when we weren't even out of high school. I'm an impatient woman, but I'm not pushing now, Deck. Someday, when you're ready, I'm hoping you'll take me to see your dad."

"I will get to that," he said. "I swear it."

"When you're ready," she said again.

They were quiet together, watching the fire.

Then he said, "And Nellie I…well, I want you to know that I'll always regret the way I treated you before. It was so wrong, what I did to you, how bad I hurt you. Twice. I am so sorry."

"I accepted your apology that first night in Vegas, remember?"

"Yeah. I do remember. I remember everything, Nellie. Every moment with you."

"I'm glad." She pulled away enough to look at him then, to hold his gaze with hers. "And I need your promise."

"Name it. Anything."

"I need your word that whatever happens in the future, we face it together. If the barrel business goes bust and Bravo Construction goes belly-up and we're barely getting by, if there's some awful family tragedy— anything, everything, whatever goes down. Deck, we have to turn *toward* each other. We can't ever let pride or fear or grief or anger win out over the love between us, over the life we're going to build together. We can't ever walk away. Do you promise?"

"I do. I promise." And he kissed her, slow and achingly, perfectly sweet. "Merry Christmas, Sparky," he said softly when he lifted his head. "I was sure you would leave me and I got hit by a car. But here we are, together, talking midsize dogs and kids, eventually. All in all, I have to call this the best Christmas I ever had."

The following Saturday, the roads were clear. Nell woke excited for the day to come. They were going to Fort Collins to see Keith McGrath.

Deck's dad welcomed them to his small apartment at the front of the complex. Keith fussed over Deck's arm and Deck said he shouldn't worry. The break was a clean one and healing well. The cast, put on just yesterday, would be off in six to eight weeks.

"Just as long as you're going to be all right," Keith said. Then he offered a simple, straightforward apology to Nell for the way he'd behaved eleven years before.

"Apology happily accepted." Nell hugged him and said how glad she was to see him doing so well.

Keith served them lunch. Once they'd eaten, he took them along a series of paths to the back of the property and around to the far side of a large parking lot. He had a workshop there. He turned on the space heater to warm things up a little and proudly showed off the kid-sized furniture and wooden toys he made.

"Someday," he said with a shy smile, "you two might be needing a few kid-sized chairs and a table to match."

Deck put his arm around Nell. "It won't be right away. But, yeah, Dad. One of these days. And a wooden train set, too."

"Anything," Keith promised with obvious pride. "Turns out I'm pretty good at this carpentry thing. If it can be made out of wood, you just tell me what you want. I'll do my best for you."

A few minutes later, Keith took them back to his place. As they approached the door, a wiry-haired brown dog stuck his head out from under a boxwood hedge.

Keith dropped to a crouch. "All right. Come on, now." The dog wiggled over and Keith scratched him behind his ears and under his chin. "You want something to eat, boy?" The dog gave a hopeful whine. "Come on inside, then." Keith held the door open and the dog led the way in.

"He got a name?" asked Deck when they were gathered in the kitchen. He held out his hand for the mutt to sniff.

"Bailey. A tenant brought him when he moved in, snuck him in, really, because he knew the complex doesn't allow pets. I warned the guy that the dog had to go. A week later, the tenant took off—skipped out on a month's rent, left Bailey here behind." Keith got out a bowl and a bag of kibble. He put down the food and then a second bowl of water. The dog got right to work on the meal. "I'd keep him. But, like I said, no pets allowed. So far, I haven't had the heart to take him to the pound. And wouldn't you know, I just seem to find myself feeding him whenever he comes around? Which happens to be pretty much every day."

Nell crouched by the dog. Bailey stopped eating long enough to wag his tail at her and lick her palm, then went right back to gobbling kibble. She glanced up at the two men standing over her.

Keith made a thoughtful sound low in his throat. "Well, now. You two wouldn't be in the market for dog, by any chance? He's a good dog, friendly. Comes when you call, knows the basic commands…"

"You can stop pitching, Dad." Deck smiled and that special dimple appeared at the corner of his mouth.

Nell rose to stand by her husband. "What do you think?"

He brushed a kiss across her upturned lips. "Looks about midsize to me."

* * * * *

The Bravo family saga continues with a whole new branch of the family!

Watch for
THE BRAVOS OF VALENTINE BAY,
*beginning May 2018,
only from Harlequin Special Edition.*

And don't miss out on previous stories in
THE BRAVOS OF JUSTICE CREEK *miniseries:*

*GARRETT BRAVO'S RUNAWAY BRIDE
THE LAWMAN'S CONVENIENT BRIDE
A BRAVO FOR CHRISTMAS
MS. BRAVO AND THE BOSS*

Available now from Harlequin Special Edition!

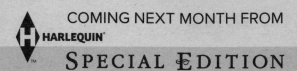

COMING NEXT MONTH FROM

HARLEQUIN®

SPECIAL EDITION

Available December 19, 2017

#2593 HER SOLDIER OF FORTUNE
The Fortunes of Texas: The Rulebreakers • by Michelle Major
When Nathan Fortune returned home, he vowed to put the past behind him. But when Bianca, his best friend's little sister, shows up with her son, Nate finds that the past won't stay buried...and it threatens to snuff out the future Nate and Bianca now hope to build with each other.

#2594 THE ARIZONA LAWMAN
Men of the West • by Stella Bagwell
Tessa Parker goes to Arizona to investigate her unexpected inheritance and gets more than a ranch. There's a sexy deputy next door and perhaps this orphan may finally find a family on the horizon.

#2595 JUST WHAT THE COWBOY NEEDED
The Bachelors of Blackwater Lake • by Teresa Southwick
Logan Hunt needs a nanny. What he gets is pretty kindergarten teacher Grace Flynn, whose desire for roots and a family flies right in the face of Logan's determination to remain a bachelor. Can Logan overcome his fears of becoming his father in time to convince Grace that she's exactly what he wants?

#2596 CLAIMING THE CAPTAIN'S BABY
American Heroes • by Rochelle Alers
Former army captain and current billionaire Giles Wainwright is shocked to learn he has a daughter and even more shocked at how attracted he is to her adoptive mother, Mya Lawson. But Mya doesn't trust Giles's motives when it comes to her heart and he will have to work harder than ever if he wants to claim Mya's love.

#2597 THE RANCHER AND THE CITY GIRL
Sweet Briar Sweethearts • by Kathy Douglass
Running for her life, Camille Parker heads to her sworn enemy, Jericho Jones, for protection. She may be safe from those who wish her harm, but as they both come to see their past presumptions proven incorrect, Camille's heart is more at risk than ever.

#2598 BAYSIDE'S MOST UNEXPECTED BRIDE
Saved by the Blog • by Kerri Carpenter
Riley Hudson is falling for her best friend and boss, Sawyer Wallace, the only person who knows she is the ubiquitous Bayside Blogger. Awkward as that could be, though, they both have bigger problems in the form of blackmail and threats to close down the newspaper they both work for! Will Sawyer see past that long enough to make Riley Bayside's most unexpected bride?

HSECNM1217

Get 2 Free Books,
Plus 2 Free Gifts—
just for trying the
Reader Service!

*When his best friend's little sister shows up with her son,
Nathan Fortune's past won't stay buried...and threatens
to snuff out the future Nate and Bianca now hope to
build with each other.*

Read on for a sneak preview of
HER SOLDIER OF FORTUNE,
the first book in the newest Fortunes continuity,
THE FORTUNES OF TEXAS:
THE RULEBREAKERS.

"He's an idiot," Nate offered automatically.

One side of her mouth kicked up. "You sound like
Eddie. He never liked Brett, even when we were first
dating. He said he wasn't good enough for me."

"Obviously that's true." Nate took a step closer
but stopped himself before he reached for her. Bianca
didn't belong to him, and he had no claim on her. But
one morning with EJ and he already felt a connection to
the boy. A connection he also wanted to explore with the
beautiful woman in front of him. "Any man who would
walk away from you needs to have his—" He paused,
feeling the unfamiliar sensation of color rising to his face.
His mother had certainly raised him better than to swear
in front of a lady, yet the thought of Bianca being hurt by
her ex made his blood boil. "He needs a swift kick in the
pants."

"Agreed," she said with a bright smile. A smile that

made him weak in the knees. He wanted to give her a reason to smile like that every day. "I'm better off without him, but it still makes me sad for EJ. I do my best, but it's hard with only the two of us. There are so many things we've had to sacrifice." She wrapped her arms around her waist and turned to gaze out of the barn, as if she couldn't bear to make eye contact with Nate any longer. "Sometimes I wish I could give him more."

"You're enough," he said, reaching out a hand to brush away the lone tear that tracked down her cheek. "Don't doubt for one second that you're enough."

As he'd imagined, her skin felt like velvet under his callused fingertip. Her eyes drifted shut and she tipped up her face, as if she craved his touch as much as he wanted to give it to her.

He wanted more from this woman—this moment— than he'd dreamed possible. A loose strand of hair brushed the back of his hand, sending shivers across his skin.

She glanced at him from beneath her lashes, but there was no hesitation in her gaze. Her liquid brown eyes held only invitation, and his entire world narrowed to the thought of kissing Bianca.

"I finished with the hay, Mommy," EJ called from behind him.

Don't miss
HER SOLDIER OF FORTUNE by Michelle Major,
available January 2018 wherever
Harlequin® Special Edition books and ebooks are sold.

www.Harlequin.com

HSEEXP1217

LOVE
Harlequin romance?

Join our Harlequin community to share your thoughts and connect with other romance readers!

Be the first to find out about promotions, news, and exclusive content!

Sign up for the Harlequin e-newsletter and download a free book from any series at

www.TryHarlequin.com

CONNECT WITH US AT:

Harlequin.com/Community

 Facebook.com/HarlequinBooks

 Twitter.com/HarlequinBooks

 Instagram.com/HarlequinBooks

 Pinterest.com/HarlequinBooks

ReaderService.com

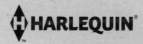 HARLEQUIN®

ROMANCE WHEN YOU NEED IT

HSOCIAL2017

THE WORLD IS BETTER WITH

Romance

Harlequin has everything from contemporary, passionate and heartwarming to suspenseful and inspirational stories.

Whatever your mood,
we have a romance just for you!

Connect with us to find your next great read,
special offers and more.

f /HarlequinBooks

y @HarlequinBooks

www.HarlequinBlog.com

www.Harlequin.com/Newsletters

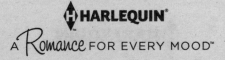

Looking for more satisfying love stories
with community and family at their core?

**Check out Harlequin® Special Edition
and Harlequin® Western Romance books!**

New books available every month!

CONNECT WITH US AT:

Harlequin.com/Community

 Facebook.com/HarlequinBooks

 Twitter.com/HarlequinBooks

 Instagram.com/HarlequinBooks

 Pinterest.com/HarlequinBooks

ReaderService.com

**ROMANCE WHEN
YOU NEED IT**

HFGENRE2017R